DEADLY SPORT

She looked up and saw lust in their pitiless faces. Their buffalo coats were so rancid that she felt her stomach flop. They grabbed her and she beat helplessly at them. They laughed and she twisted free and threw herself into the swirling water, clawing to reach the swiftness of the current. Fingers locked into her hair and her face was shoved deep into the mud. She choked and swallowed water. A silent scream filled her chest as she was torn from the mud and the river.

All was lost. Her eyes and her mouth were filled with mud and she was dying, unable to breathe.

"She's chokin' to death, Zeb! Dunk her face again!"

Other *Leisure* books by Gary McCarthy:
POWDER RIVER
WIND RIVER

SODBUSTER

GARY McCARTHY

LEISURE BOOKS NEW YORK CITY

for
Joe Matacia
who also rode south

A LEISURE BOOK®

December 1998

Published by

Dorchester Publishing Co., Inc.
276 Fifth Avenue
New York, NY 10001

ISBN 0-8439-4467-6

The name "Leisure Books" and the stylized "L" with design are trademarks of Dorchester Publishing Co., Inc.

Printed in the United States of America.

Chapter One

Zachariah Bennett awoke with such a sense of emptiness that he squeezed his eyes tightly together and tried to force himself back to sleep. But after a few minutes, he gave up and stared into the pre-dawn darkness, knowing that he would make a fool of himself tomorrow when he stood up to make a graduation speech, a speech he could not even think of how to begin. And even if, by some miracle, he survived that experience, Zack knew his fate was sealed. After all the years of schooling, of dreaming, he would then become a full-time sodbuster—probably forever.

Zack could hear old Red Rooster crowing high above their sod house. It was a miracle that the coyotes had not eaten it along with all their other chickens. But Red Rooster was especially wary and could fly like a crow. Still, it would have been long gone if Zack had not set a tall pole in their grass-covered roof. Since there were no trees for miles around, the pole was the rooster's salvation, even though, in winter when the wind blew hard across Wyoming, it bent like a bow and the bird would have fits trying to cling to its ice-crusted arms. Zack's mother always took pity on the rooster and brought it inside to thaw out during the worst of the storms.

Rescuing that rooster always started a quarrel between Ma and Pa. Adolph Bennett wanted to eat the rooster, not save it. But since the rooster cost them no feed, living off bugs and whatever it would find, Adolph allowed it to exist. Besides, even Pa had to admit that Red Rooster was too scrawny to be worth the plucking. Saving that rooster was the only thing Zack's mother had ever stood up and fought for. And that was why, whenever Zack awoke to hear coyotes on their roof circling the perched red rooster and chewing at the slender wooden pole, he would race out and chase the coyotes away. But one of these days, Zack thought, I will just let the coyotes chew through the wood and bring that rooster down. To escape a pack of hungry coyotes, the rooster would have to fly all the way to Cheyenne. That was fifteen miles and Zack didn't think the rooster was bird enough to do it.

Carrie reached out and touched his shoulder. She was seventeen, and whenever she touched him in the dark, Zack recoiled with embarrassment. Carrie was a woman, and he was mighty close to being a man.

"You awake, Zack?"

"Yeah."

"You thought up a speech yet?"

"No." The speech was a sore point between them.

8

Last year, Carrie also had won top honors and she had given a dandy. Zack knew there was no chance that he could equal her speech, but everyone was expecting him to. Carrie was a better talker and she was a whole lot smarter. Just like Ma was smarter than Pa in learning and putting thoughts into fine words—unless you were talking about those from the Bible. When it came to the Bible, Pa could outquote anyone except a preacher. That was all the more amazing since he could not read or write. But he had been read to so much as a child that the knowledge of the scriptures was an indelible part of his mind.

Carrie's straw mattress crunched as she rolled over on her elbow and stared at her younger brother. "Well, you better. Miss Newby isn't going to be happy if you go tongue-tied in front of everyone. You'll never live down that shame, Zack!"

"If you'd shut up, maybe I could think of something right now."

"No, you won't. I think you had better let me find the time to write something up for you today."

"Uh-uh," he said. "I got to do it myself."

"Then you better . . ."

"You children hush and get up now!" Adolph growled.

Their soddie was twenty feet deep into the hill and thirty-three feet wide. It was one room but, at night, Ma hung a sheet of thin muslin between herself and Pa and the children. So now Zack could see the glimmering outline of his father as Adolph stood and scratched his lean frame and then fumbled for his dirt-encrusted overalls. Adolph was the tallest and skinniest man for miles around and Zack guessed he'd be pretty tall himself one day.

"Carrie, your mother is feeling poorly again. Git up and fix something to eat. Zachariah, we still got four acres of bad weeds to hoe. The Good Lord only helps those that help themselves. Git up, boy! We can get one of 'em done before we eat and go to the Slater place."

Zack nodded. He reached down and pulled on his pants under the covers, threw his legs out of bed and slipped into a canvas shirt that was stiff from dried sweat and mud. He knuckled the sleep from his eyes and hurried to the water barrel where he dipped a scoop of creek water. Carrie stumbled up and drank as soon as he had his fill. A trickle of dirt showered down through the muslin that hung from the ceiling. Zack guessed that the cow was on the roof again. It seemed to prefer that little patch of earth to anything else on their entire 160 acres of homesteaded land.

Zack heard the leather door hinges squeak and then he felt the soft caress of the morning air. The days were already getting hot. Adolph had to crouch in the doorway and his wide rack of shoulders filled it completely, though he stood cockeyed. A fall from a mule had broken his left shoulder so that he tipped that way. He was always in pain, though it was worse when the weather was cold.

"Come on, you two!" he grumbled sternly as he stepped outside.

Adolph walked three paces out into the yard and dropped to his knees. He bowed his head in prayer but waited until Zack and Carrie were kneeling beside him before beginning the daily ritual.

"Oh Lord," Adolph began, his face lifted to the burning sunrise so that his spiky whiskers gleamed like red nettles, ''we ask you to protect us from Indians and locust, from devil cattlemen and from all kinds of other pestilence. We are your people, doin' your will as best that we can. We need a good rain pretty bad, Lord, for the winter wheat standing in our fields. Give us the strength to earn our daily bread and to think clean and wholesome thoughts so that we will not burn in hell through all eternity. *Thy* will be done and not that of us dreadful sinners. Amen.''

Adolph lowered his head. ''Carrie?'' he whispered, not even turning to look at her.

Zack held his breath because, early in the morning like this, Carrie got foolish with herself and might say anything.

''I pray that Zack will think of some good words for his graduation tomorrow and that there will be cookies and milk at the schoolhouse like last year and that Billy . . .''

The back of Adolph's massive hand struck her across the cheek hard enough that the rooster, who had been listening closely, squawked and flew off his pole.

Zack's fists clenched at his sides and he forgot about the Lord as he was gripped by a mixture of hate and confusion. He knew the blow had sounded worse than it had felt, but Pa was way too hard on Carrie and hitting her only made her hate him all the more. Zack looked at his sister, knowing he would never understand why Carrie dared to provoke their father. It scared him and made him feel guilty, too. Carrie was smallish like Ma, but she had more steel in her than any three grown women. That was why, although Zack towered over her by a full head, Carrie made him feel proud and guilty at the same time.

"You know that ain't no way to pray!" Adolph said harshly. "Zachariah, *you* give us a prayer."

Zack searched for the words and the courage to defy his father like Carrie. But he couldn't. He was more scared of Pa even than of God. And though he would never admit it—not even to Carrie—praying seemed mostly a waste of time. The Lord sure hadn't made Pa any nicer toward the family. If the Lord was really watching over the Bennett flock, he'd have kilt Pa and they'd all have gone back to St. Louis where life was a sight easier.

"Zachariah!"

His lips spit out the same old words his Pa liked to hear recited again and again. "I pray for a good crop of wheat this year, potatoes and maybe a little corn, too, for meal and johnny cakes and especially for good wheat prices this fall. I pray for summer rain and that no Sioux Indians will come by and steal or shoot our milk cow or steal the mules like they did last year. And I pray for Ma and her health and that we strike well water real soon."

Adolph nodded with stern approval. "That's good prayin', Zachariah. The Lord will take note that you don't make sport of it like your prideful sister."

"She's all right, Pa. She meant no sinfulness."

Adolph's face hardened and sunrise burned it red. "I'll be the judge of that. Now, let's git to the fields and the work."

They took their hoes and got busy. The morning was the best time of day, though Zack's muscles protested with each swing of the hoe. He was sixteen, and though

12

not yet much over six feet tall, he was heavier than his father and suspected that he was as strong. Because of that, he forced himself to match chops with the hoe with Pa, but he tired easier and could not keep up the pace for over an hour at a stretch.

The winter corn was up three or four inches in most places. There had been little spring rain, and if the plants did not get some moisture soon, they would wither and die. But weeds seemed to prosper in the rich, dark soil, and if it were not for the wheat, a blind man could have weeded the fields as well as a sighted one.

Zack felt the first trickle of sweat dribble down between his shoulder blades to slide along his spine. He watched the big orb of the sun float up over the horizon and the clouds to the east lose their lacy pink linings. The land rolled like a green sea of grass and seemed to go on forever. He had heard that the land was flat as a tabletop in Kansas and Nebraska. Zack was glad that was not true in this southeastern corner of Wyoming. He had heard that flat land could drive a body crazy because the earth seemed so endless and empty. But with hills, it was not so stark and monotonous.

Anyway, he thought, Cheyenne is only fifteen miles away and so is the Union Pacific Railroad. Pa hated all railroads. They had tricked him into buying acreage in Kansas back in 1869 with the promise of good land cheap and with no money down, only two-fifty an acre, and you paid just the interest for the first three years. That's what all the railroad fliers said. Some even offered to refund your train tickets west if you bought their land. Thousands of folk had bought land just like Pa but most were soon gone. Zack had been old enough to remember the repossession men coming and taking all of

Ma's furniture, their livestock, wagons and even the corn and potatoes they had stored in the root cellar.

The family had walked away with nothing but bitterness and the clothes they wore. That's why they'd come to Wyoming and homesteaded. At least here, if you could build a house, dig a good well and survive five years, the land was yours. And maybe just as important, if you failed, no railroad or bank could take what you owned. You could just walk away. Lots of folks did. But more and more were coming, so that even the big cattlemen and the cowboys were starting to worry.

Pa hated railroads even more than he hated cattlemen. He said it was thievery, the way they'd taken that land from the public and then sold it right back to them. The railroads were run by Godless men. But to Zack's way of thinking, Pa seemed to think that anyone with enough money to spend on fancy things was Godless. He was always quoting the scripture about it being harder for a rich man to get into heaven than for a camel to pass through the eye of a needle. Because most railroad men and cattle ranchers were rich and you never saw them living in sod houses, Pa called them all sinners.

"What's taking Carrie so long with breakfast!" Adolph complained, finally stopping to lean on his hoe and wipe sweat from his face. "Sometimes I swear that the Lord made womenfolk just to test the patience of a man. Trouble is, I spoilt Carrie the same way I spoilt your Ma."

"Ma isn't spoiled," Zack said, unwilling to allow such a statement to pass. "She's just sick and worn down."

"Well, *I'm* worn down, too! But I'll outwork any man you'll ever hoe a field beside."

But you aren't sick, Zack thought, as he turned to look back at the sod house. The door was open and a veil of blue smoke was coming out of it, before curling up to join the bigger stream coming from the smokestack of their Franklin stove. Zack could smell potatoes frying and he wished they could afford some meat, but they could not. Carrie would be tossing cow chips into the Franklin from the box she used to collect them every afternoon. The darned things burned so fast that it took at least thirty or forty just for one meal.

"Ma has never been strong," his father said. "I guess we all know that."

"Carrie's the one who helps her the most."

"She's got a sassy tongue and a willful nature about her that tells me that the devil dances with her mind."

Zack lifted his hoe and attacked the weeds until his father did the same. There was no sense talking to him about Carrie. Pa's mind was set. Carrie couldn't have pleased him with a new shirt on Christmas.

The potatoes were burned, but everyone was so hungry not a word passed among them as they ate their fill. As soon as they had finished washing down their food with water, Pa got up and said, "Zack, it'll be nine o'clock before we get to Slater's place and start on that new room. They are gonna be mad at us for bein' so tardy."

Zack went over and looked down at his mother who still had not gotten up. She looked as old as Grandma had the day she died. Like Pa, she was way too thin and the only time she seemed happy was when she and Carrie were working together in the house, or when she was out in her garden admiring the few flowers that Pa allowed her to plant between the rows of corn and squash.

"You rest easy," he said.

She squeezed his hand. "You don't let them work you too hard, Zack. Tomorrow is special and I don't want you to doze off in church or at the school party later."

"I won't, Ma."

"Carrie tells me you ain't got a word of that speech in your mind."

Zack shook his head. "I'll think of it today, I reckon."

"Maybe Carrie will write you up a few lines."

"I can do my own." He turned and headed for the pen where Pa kept their two oxen, but before he stepped outside, he turned to Carrie and said, "I'll think of the words myself, Carrie."

"Won't hurt to have a few extra, will it?"

He paused and finally replied, "I reckon not. Long as they sound like my own."

"They will," she promised.

Zack nodded, and when he passed outdoors and walked toward the ox pen, he felt a whole lot better, almost as if a ton of sod had been lifted from his back. Sometimes a man had to let good sense get the best of foolish pride. Carrie's words would be a lot finer.

Slater's place was five miles down the road beside the same Lodgepole Creek that passed within a quarter of a mile of their own homestead. And as they rode their old wagon along behind the oxen, Zack could see the tiny specks of a cattle herd and he wished he could go watch the cowboys at work. It was spring roundup and he knew that they would be sweeping the prairie for newborn calves to rope and brand. Zack had never seen a roundup, but he'd met someone who had. It sounded like a whole lot more fun than building a room addition for

Elmer Slater. Zack didn't know anything about *real* cattle, only milk cows, and they bore no resemblance to the Texas longhorns that had replaced the buffalo on this range during the last twenty years. In truth, Zack knew that it was not the cattle themselves that was so inviting, but the life of the men who tended them. Cowboys never shuffled along barefooted behind the plow; in fact, they almost never touched the earth with the soles of their boots unless it was to eat, relieve themselves or go into a saloon and howl. But a sodbuster worked in the dirt until it became a part of his skin and he could never wash it from his feet, his hands or the back of his neck.

That was another thing Zack would never confess to anyone, not even Carrie. If he'd been given the choice, Zack guessed he'd have been a cowboy. And sometimes, when he saw them loping across the prairie, he felt as hopeless as that rooster must when it looked down at a pack of coyotes gnawing on its perch-pole. He felt as if he was just postponing the inevitable. But there was Carrie and Ma and that damned scrawny rooster and they all needed him like this cracked earth needed a good drenching rain.

When the restlessness grew too strong, he walked to the tallest hill on their section, and if it was night, he could see the lights of Cheyenne. They winked so prettily you'd think that a basketful of stars had tumbled out of God's hand to rest on the black prairie.

Pa did not like Cheyenne, of course. He swore it was the devil's playground, and maybe he was right, for Zack knew there was drunkenness and painted ladies, though he was not sure what they did—exactly. Every Sunday the family went to church, with Pa dressed in his old black suit and hat and his shoes that had holes the size of twenty-dollar gold pieces in their soles. And Ma, she put on her one decent dress and that sad old hat she had got for her wedding so long ago, and she went to sing in the choir with the other wives who dressed about the same.

It was a good thing that Pa was so set with God that he never missed a Sunday service. If not for church and the singing, Ma would have gone crazy and died a long time ago. And after church, if there were no cowboys around drunk from Saturday night and set on raising hell, then the sodbusters and their families might walk down to Fulton's Grocery and buy a stick of peppermint candy along with the other provisions they needed. But that was only if they had money, and ever since last year, the sodbusters had been dead broke. It had been so long since Pa let Ma buy peppermint or licorice that Zack had forgotten what it tasted like.

Elmer Slater was a cross-tempered, square-built man with a red nose. You could map the blue veins on it from across the room and his eyes were the closest and most deepest that Zack had ever seen. He stood under five and a half feet tall, yet his shoulders and arms were so thick he looked as if he could harness himself up to the special grasshopper plow and cut the long strips of sod all by himself. But Elmer claimed to have such a sore back that he rarely dared lift anything heavier than a heaping plate of his wife's cooking. He was ten years younger than Pa and already was near useless for heavy work. His wife and his brood of eight freckled children did almost everything while Elmer drove the plow or wagon.

Zack and his father had worked off and on for Elmer

Slater for two years. He never paid them in cash money but bartered instead, as most of the sodbusters were wont to do. For this big house addition and a storage shed for grain and farm equipment, Elmer would give them the two oxen and the grasshopper plow, so that they could find employment with the growing number of new arrivals eager to have their try at farming the land.

Pa was excited about the deal. To his way of thinking, the oxen and the plow would make it certain that, even if their wheat crop failed, they would never go hungry as long as there were folks desperate enough to be sodbusters. Sod was free, but to take it, a man needed more than a shovel and a wheelbarrow. Even a small house took almost an acre of sod and that was a lot by any man's standard. The Slater's room addition was bigger than the entire Bennett house, and coupled with the storage shed, it would take almost three and a half acres of sod to finish the building.

"We'll finish this up by the end of next month, and then you wait and see," Pa said. "All we got to do is drive these big oxen around with the plow on our wagon and the people will come running to us, begging us to do their work."

"Lots of people have mules."

"Sure, but a mule won't pull as straight a line or as deep," Pa grunted. "These plows cost thirty dollars. I reckon that's more than it'll cost 'em for the sod they'll need."

"What about the wheat?" Zack looked at his father. "I thought we were going to start threshing it in August."

"We will. Need be, we can cut sod by the moon and

cut wheat by the sun. Might earn us about seventy-five or eighty dollars.''

Zack turned away and said nothing. For a man who condemned the rich, sometimes it seemed as if his Pa spent a lot of time tallying up dollar figures. ''Ma wants an extra window for our house,'' he said. ''She needs the sunlight real bad. The stove is near burnt out, too. And neither she nor Carrie have a decent church dress and . . .''

''Stove and one window will do her fine. One window is all she needs to see by. They can have some calico cloth if the wheat prices are up.'' He shook his head in disgust. ''I swear that everyone in this family is wantin' some fancy thing or the other.''

Zack let it alone and said nothing more the rest of the day. He worked the oxen and handled the grasshopper plow which cut the sod into strips about fourteen inches wide and three deep. It rolled the sod over so that the roots were facing the sky. Then along came Pa with a broadax to cut the strips into three-foot sections, light enough to lift onto their groaning old wagon bed. When they had cut all they'd need for a few hours, they'd take them back to the soddie and stack them two wide and overlapping end to end. That way, the walls would be better than two feet thick.

But the plowing went slowly. Without a rain in three weeks, the earth was hard and unyielding. Yet the huge oxen were so powerful and the grasshopper plow so sharp, they made steady progress throughout the long day. About an hour short of sundown, the afternoon wind began to kick up great clouds of dust from the long, freshly shorn strips of bare land. They hurried to finish the east wall, lapping it with the north one and tying it all together by driving a stake down through both ends. It was simple but hard work, and as the day wore on, the sod strips seemed to grow heavier and heavier. Zack took the worst of it by unloading the wagon and carrying the sod over to his father for placement. Even so, he could tell his Pa was laboring hard. Watching him strain and noting the fatigue etched deep into every line of his face, Zack was reminded that his father was growing old before his natural time. The man's hair was pure white. Ten years ago, there had been heavy ropes of muscle in his back, arms and shoulders, but now there were only thin strings that stood out whenever he lifted a patch of sod.

Elmer Slater, fat and resting comfortably in the shade of his new wall must have noticed it too, for he said, "How old are you, Adolph?"

"Forty-one." Adolph did not even stop to glance down at the man as he set the wall, strip by heavy strip, grass down, edges butted together tight enough to keep out the wind.

Slater clucked his tongue like a gossipy old woman. "You look a sight older. Hell, I'm only thirty-one."

"I know. You told me," Adolph grunted as he slammed down another strip and used the heel of his palm to drive it into the next one real tight.

"You ought to slow down a little. You work too damned hard. It's catching up with you."

Adolph placed his hands on the small of his back and straightened. For just an instant, pain leapt into his eyes. But when it passed, he yanked out his handkerchief and wiped the back of his neck, then his arms and finally his face. The sweat and the dirt smeared into black mud. He studied the sod walls carefully and Zack could tell he was mostly concerned about the window and doorway they'd worked on earlier. In this treeless land, precious wood beams had been used to block their openings. The great weight of the sod roof would cause it to settle three or four inches during the first year. Knowing this, Adolph had left that much of a gap over the window and door. If you forgot to do that, the glass windows and even solid wooden doors would buckle and snap like dry sticks.

No one could have been more surprised than Zack when his father said, "My boy is going to graduate tomorrow and give a speech after church."

"Oh?" Elmer glanced at Zack and he sounded more critical than impressed. "Mighty big boy to go to school so long."

"He's sixteen," Adolph said almost apologetically. "It's long past time he worked like a man. He sure eats like one."

"It shows," Slater said. "He's not so skinny as you, either. You pretty strong, are you, Zack?"

Zack flushed with embarrassment. He understood Pa would want him to be humble and say, "No, I am not."

"Sorta," Zack said, knowing how much his response would have pleased Carrie. But his response did not sit well with either man.

"Well, you oughta be," Elmer grunted. "You're bigger than a lot of growed men already. You shoulda been helping your father since three years ago."

"I told his Ma that," Adolph said, encouraged at finding a man whose views corresponded so closely with his own. "But she was stubborn about him and Carrie going all the way through school. Used her own inheritance money to pay for the loss of wages."

22

Zack turned away in shame. He had not known that fact until this year or he'd have quit school sooner.

"Women get funny ideas," Elmer was saying. "You want a glass of cold well water?"

Zack would have liked it, but his father said no. They would let the oxen drink in the creek while washing themselves clean for dinner tonight and church in the morning. Pa believed that a man needed to be both clean of mind and body before he could enter church.

"Reckon Zachariah is done in," Adolph said as he climbed down and headed for the wagon with Zack right behind. "We'll be leaving now."

"But you still got another fifteen or twenty minutes of good daylight," Slater complained. But when Pa kept walking and then climbed into the wagon, he glumly added, "Well, then, see you tomorrow."

"Not on the Sabbath," Adolph shouted as he wheeled the oxen around in the yard and pointed them up the road toward home.

"Then on Monday!"

Elmer sounded mighty disgusted to Zack and maybe he was. Neither the man nor his wife or children went to church. Because of that, they lived mostly without friends and yet they seemed a lot better off than their neighbors. They had another team of oxen, a fine sod house soon to be even finer, two wagons and plenty of cows, chickens and pigs. All that and a brand new Halladay Standard windmill imported clear from Batavia, Illinois, that probably cost a hundred dollars and could draw that many gallons of water each day. Meanwhile, Zack and his father had to tote their life-giving water from Lodgepole Creek almost a quarter mile away. It had made Zack consider more than once the dubious value of being a prayerful family.

It wasn't fifteen minutes later that they both turned and saw the cowboys. There were two of them and they were galloping up fast behind them along the same creek road. Zack had seen them like this on a hundred Saturday nights and there was little doubt they were heading for the saloons and dancehall girls in Cheyenne. It was growing dusk, and in the poor light, Zack could not see them well, but he could sure hear them shouting.

"Sodbusters! Yee-haw! Move outa our way, you land-grabbin' buzzards!"

Pa grabbed his whip but he did not use it, yet. "Turn back around and ignore them, Zachariah!"

"But Pa, I think you'd best pull off the road a ways."

"This ain't their private road. They can ride around," Adolph said through clenched teeth.

Zack dared to glance around just in time to see the cowboys sweep past on both sides of their yoke of oxen with their twirling ropes. They were laughing and their aims were true as their ropes settled over the big oxen. They dallied their ropes around their saddle horns and reined sharply off the road. They spurred hard.

The oxen bawled as the ropes cut into their tender throats. They yielded to the pressure and stumbled off the road, swinging their big heads and choking like babies. The wagon bounced so hard into the field that it almost unseated Zack.

"Let loose of my oxen!" his father shouted, lashing out at the cowboys while pulling the oxen back toward the road again.

"Whoo-weee!" one cowboy yelled, discovering that

24

the two cow ponies were no match for oxen in a pulling contest. "Those sonsabitches are strong! Look out, old man, you hit me and . . ."

Adolph's whip lashed his cheek and split it open. The cowboy cursed and threw off his rope. Even in bad light, the wound looked ugly and all the fun and hoorahing went right out of the pair. When Adolph started to lash the man again, the second cowboy spurred his horse in close and threw himself into the wagon. Zack saw him coming and managed to drive a fist against the cowboy's jaw, but the man was so infuriated he still was able to grab the stock whip and then get in a couple of good punches.

Zack grabbed him around the neck and tried to throw him off the wagon. His father was shouting and striking back so hard the cowboy was knocked clean off the wagon and then the iron wheels rolled over his leg and he screamed hideously.

Adolph grabbed for the lines, but it was too late as the rear wheels crushed the cowboy's other leg. Zack flew off the wagon, knowing that he was too late to do anything. He knelt beside the man but the other cowboy came running up. His cheek was bleeding and he clamped a hand on Zack's shoulder, fingers biting deep into flesh. He tore Zack aside and knelt beside his friend who was screaming in pain.

"Sodbuster, you tried to kill him!" he yelled, twisting his face up toward Adolph and drawing his gun. When he started to pull the trigger, Zack threw himself at the man. The gun exploded and a bullet ate into the wagon-bed. The cowboy was insane with fury but he was smallish and Zack had every advantage except experience. When the cowboy tried to turn his gun and kill him,

Zack sledged him in the face with his fist. The man's nose broke with a sickening pop and then Adolph landed on the road and began kicking the cowboy in the head. His father had always possessed an insane temper, but this was the first time Zack had seen Pa actually want to kill.

"No, Pa!" Zack shouted, tearing the gun away from the cowboy and then hurling it into the brush. He grabbed his father around the ankles and they went down struggling; it took all of Zack's strength to hold him until his fury subsided.

The cowboy with the crushed legs was delirious with pain, but the other one spat blood and his eyes were wild with hatred. "You bloody sodbusters are gonna pay for this!" he shouted, jabbing a finger at them. "I swear you will!"

"It was an accident," Zack pleaded, grabbing the oxen and starting to tear their yokes off them.

"What are you gonna do!" Adolph demanded.

"We gotta get him to a doctor, Pa!"

Adolph grabbed his whip and brought it slashing down across Zack's shoulders. It felt like a knife blade cutting him to the bone. Zack fell back and the whip came down again. "Git in the wagon," he shouted. "Git!"

Covering his face as more blows lashed down, Zack jumped up into the wagon and then his father was grabbing the cowboys' ropes and tearing them free of the oxen. A moment later, he was whipping the huge animals into a stumbling trot.

Zack sat on the wagon seat and looked back at the two cowboys. The one whose nose he hadn't really meant to break was cradling the other in his lap. Their cow ponies were grazing close by.

"Pa, you should have let me put their horses in harness and gotten that man with the broken legs to a doctor in Cheyenne!"

"To hell with them heathen bastards!" Adolph glanced back over his shoulder. In the rising moonlight, his face looked sick and pale, but his words throbbed with conviction. "Justice is swift for the sinner!"

Zack stared back at the two hurt cowboys until darkness and distance blocked out the sight. Then, he turned around toward the faint yellow rectangle of light that signaled their sod house just a few miles away. *Maybe*, he thought with a growing sense of dread, *justice was also going to be swift for us sodbusters*.

Chapter Two

Nothing had been said about the cowboys, not last night when they got home or later over a dinner of corn meal and boiled potatoes. Zack had kept waiting for his father to bring up the subject, but the man hadn't said a word. It was almost as if . . . as if saying nothing would make it seem as if it had not happened.

But it *had* happened, Zack thought, as he stood out in their farmyard and listened to the sounds of the night. And sure as angels wore wings, cowboys would come for him and his Pa before tomorrow's daylight. There was nothing to stop them because, no matter what their preacher or anyone else who sided with the farmers said, Wyoming was and always would be cattle country. Ranchers were more powerful than any ragged collection of sodbusters. And if those ranchers and their wild cowboys wanted to, Zack knew they could lynch him and Pa on a single rope thrown over a telegraph pole. No one would dare stop them.

Zack dug his toes into the thick carpet of buffalo grass. He looked up at the blaze of stars and wondered if he ought to get his father's rifle and go stand watch on the hilltop until morning. He wished Pa hadn't lost his temper and shot their dog last year for killing a chicken; a dog would at least give them some warning. But even with a warning, what chance would they have against a gang of gun-toting cowboys? None.

They'll shoot the livestock, he thought miserably. And without the oxen and the milk cow, we are finished. But there isn't even any place to hide the cow out here. There is just nowhere to run except to the willows along Lodgepole Creek, and that's the first place they'd look.

"Zack?"

He turned around to see Carrie come sneaking out of the soddie. She was dressed in a long old nightgown, the one that had belonged to Pa but that Ma had shortened. And though she was fully matured and altogether a woman, she seemed like a little girl as she tiptoed across their yard in the moonlight. Zack wondered if the cowboys would hurt her, too, or just let her watch the hanging. He wished she lived someplace else. Pa didn't like her and a poor dirt farm in this godforsaken part of Wyoming was sure no place for a woman who wanted any kind of life. Carrie had too much sparkle to let the prairie dust grind her down as it had Ma. She was a really pretty girl.

"What are you doing out here all alone?" She took his arm. "What's wrong with you tonight?"

"Nothin'."

"Yes, there is!" she whispered sharply. "I can tell

and so could Ma if she wasn't feeling so poorly. Now, tell me! Is it something Mr. Slater did? He can be mighty sharp-tongued and you just have to . . .''

"It wasn't Mr. Slater," Zack said. He knew Carrie would not let him alone until she heard the whole awful story, so he said, "I'm going up to sit on our burying hill. You wanna come, I guess I'll talk."

Carrie nodded and came along. They moved through their wheat field, being careful not to step on the young plants. Pa would come out in the morning, and in just one glance, would see one crushed plant in ten thousand and know what caused the damage.

They climbed the low, grassy hill and sat down beside the graves of little Peter and Jerome Bennett, neither of whom had lived long enough to make their absence a sharp pain. They faced Cheyenne and Zack gazed at the distant lights. He wished he could leave home and he knew that Carrie felt the same.

"Well, what is it, Zack!" Carrie had waited all evening for the meal to be finished, then for the dishes and the Bible reading. She had scrubbed the pans and washed the tabletop, plates and eating utensils, expecting any minute that either her father or Zack would speak about the thing that obviously had gone wrong. But like a couple of mutes, they hadn't said a word and so they had all gone to bed. The minute Pa began to snore, Zack had gone outside. That's when Carrie had had enough of this silent nonsense and decided to put the issue to him straight-out.

Zack cleared his throat. "We had a bad run-in with two cowboys coming home," he began.

And while Carrie sat quietly, he told the story clear and clean, without a lot of extra words, which, as far as

Carrie was concerned, was one of his finest qualities. Most men, Pa included, were just too damn windy. Most women, Ma excluded, were, too. But at least women had a reason—out in this awful country, they saw each other so infrequently and then for such short periods that they had to talk fast to get through with everything they needed saying. All that *had* to be said or they'd go crazy and start talking to themselves. Carrie had seen that happen way too often not to know it was true.

When Zack was finished, Carrie leaned forward so that her chin was on her forearms as they rested on her bent knees. "So Pa crippled one and almost kicked the other one's brains out, huh?"

"He sorta went crazy when the man pulled his gun and tried to shoot him."

"Pa *is* crazy," Carrie said. "The Bible made him that way. He lives two thousand years ago with Jesus, only nothing is the same now and Jesus doesn't speak to him. Satan has got in the way. I won't read him the Bible and Ma can't read."

"Then why don't he just ask *me* to do it?"

" 'Cause he considers it woman's work. I heard him say one time that it is fine to read the Bible and pray, but it is wrong for one man to be read to by another. Said it was unnatural."

"I don't understand that."

"It's just his craziness," Carrie said. "And some of it spilled over this evening and we don't know what's going to become of us now. It's sorta exciting, don't you think?"

He turned and stared at her in disbelief. "It isn't exciting to me! I might get hung."

"Not likely," Carrie said. "All you did was get in a

31

lucky lick and break a man's nose. Pa did the bad damage.''

Zack turned back to study the lights of Cheyenne. There was enough truth in his sister's words to give him some comfort, though it also brought a guilty feeling. ''I'll stand with Pa one way or the other,'' he said, trying to ease his conscience.

''Even under a hangman's noose?''

Carrie was almost smiling. That made Zack angry. ''Yeah, if I had to!''

''Then you'd be crazy as Pa,'' she said, the smile dying on her lips and a furrow creasing her forehead. ''Zack, promise me you won't be that crazy. I need you and Ma needs us both.''

''Who does Pa need?''

''Jesus in heaven, before his devil-fury kills somebody here on earth.''

''And who do I need?''

''Nobody—yet. But you will someday.''

''No, I won't. I'm going to be a cowboy and ride free. They don't need nobody.''

''The hell they don't,'' Carrie said. ''They need whores that remind them of their childhood sweethearts.''

''Carrie!'' Zack was shocked at such thinking and downright embarrassed at his sister.

She threw back her head and laughed. Shocking Zack was the only real pleasure she had in life. But it had a purpose, too—maybe if she shocked him often enough, maybe he wouldn't take life so seriously.

''You ought to be ashamed of yourself,'' Zack said, not caring that he sounded angry.

''Would you feel any better if I said I was ashamed?''

"I think I might," he ventured.

Carrie laughed softly this time. "All right, then I *do* feel ashamed. And sleepy. Let's go inside and go to bed."

"I can't. They might come for us in the night."

"Then what would it matter?"

Her thoughts mirrored his own. If a bunch of cowboys intent on rope justice were coming, then they were coming, and it didn't much matter if the two oldest Bennett children were awake or asleep. But even so, something inside wanted to meet them out here under the stars. The idea of them bursting into the house and having Ma start crying was too much to bear. It would keep him awake for sure.

"None, I guess. But I am stayin' here all the same."

Carrie flopped back on the grass with a sigh. She had long, straw-colored hair and the same oval face as her mother. It was just that the day-to-day living in a soddie quickly robbed a woman of her prettiness. Right now, her nightshirt was twisted a little so that Zack could see the full outline of her breasts. Even the nipples. It bothered him so much that he turned away from her and closed his eyes and asked God for forgiveness. But then, even while he prayed—his mind betrayed him and jumped to the whores in Cheyenne. A man could not miss them. They made his mouth feel dry and his heart beat itself to pieces against the inside of his ribs. But they were messengers of the devil, he knew Pa was right about that much. Maybe that was why Carrie had said that the cowboys visited them because they reminded them of their sweethearts. Only Satan himself could be that lowdown.

"What are you thinking about?"

Zack told a half-truth. "About Cheyenne and cowboys. You think I'd make a good one?"

Carrie detected the desperation in his voice. It was a question that he had asked her dozens of times, mostly in the same way. It was nice to tell the truth and help him at the same time. "I'm the one who used to sneak out with you at night last summer and help you catch and ride the milk cow, remember?"

"Yeah. I rode it pretty good, didn't I?" The memory was one of the few good ones he held.

"Just like a bronc rider. You have a natural flair for being a cowboy, Zack. I know you'll be a great one."

He turned, smiling at her so happily she wanted to weep because he was losing that boyishness that she loved so much.

"All I need is boots and a hat. Maybe some Levi's instead of these patched-up bib overalls."

"And a red bandanna," she added, "and a leather belt instead of a piece of rope."

"Of course," he said, his eyes drifting off toward the distant lights. "If I was dressed thataway, I could stand among them and they'd never know I was a sodbuster."

"You're better than most of them," Carrie said, suddenly going serious. "A lot better."

He scratched the mosquito bites that covered his bare ankles where he always got them because his pants were too short. "No, I ain't," he said quietly.

Carrie sat up and she consciously avoided touching him because that would bring him out of his little reverie. She gave him several minutes and then said, "Listen, sodbuster, tomorrow you graduate and you haven't given a thought to that speech of yours, have you?"

"Not much."

"Then I want you to repeat it after me."

"You memorized one?" He was flabbergasted that she'd do such a hard thing.

"Sure! And so will you. Now pay attention and let's get this finished and then sleep under these stars. If the cowboys come by and shoot us dead, at least we'll have a straight flight to heaven without having to go through a roof or anything."

Zack shook his head in amazement. Carrie had a strange way of looking at things, but she was still pretty darned smart.

Zack awoke at daybreak, red-eyed and stiff-muscled but very grateful simply to be alive. After mastering Carrie's speech, he had spent the early morning hours dreaming of longhorn cattle and cowboys. Only his dreams were sour and fearful, and instead of roping a steer cleanly as he had dreamed in all times past, this time the lariat that he threw had missed the sweeping horns of a steer and then come back to fasten itself around his own neck. It had chocked him into a strangling wakefulness.

Twice, Carrie had touched his cheek and held his hand until he had pulled it away with embarrassment. But now, Carrie was gone and there was nothing around him but dew-glistening, grassy plains. Zack watched the daylight cover the land; it melted and flowed across the prairie like hot butter. Pregnant with heat, the sun struggled off the eastern horizon. There were no rain clouds, only the high, wispy kind that sailed like feathers in the wind.

Zack turned away from Cheyenne and studied their field of wheat. Even in the shadowy places, the plants seemed wilted and small. The preacher had better start praying harder for rain.

Red Rooster crowed once more, then glided off its pole and landed badly, feet-first but then crashing onto its beak and tumbling with a loud and indignant cackle. Jim the mule, Sadie, their milk cow, and Mr. Slater's oxen watched from their pen. It seemed a shame that, with so much prairie, they had to feed livestock cut grass, but if allowed to roam unattended, they'd devour the wheat plants and leave the buffalo grass untouched.

Zack climbed to his feet, brushed off the seat of his bib overalls and headed for Lodgepole Creek and a bath. Last night, they'd forgotten to take one and he guessed Pa would go to church dirty. Zack moved through the willows, watching closely for water snakes and duck eggs but saw neither. When he had stepped out of his work clothes, he wasted no time wading into the creek and was not surprised to discover that the water was colder than the still morning air. When he had drunk his fill, he took a handful of fine sand and scrubbed himself, then used marsh grass to dry. Usually, he had clean clothes to change into on Sunday, but not this morning. Zack had a feeling that nothing was going to go right this day. Not his speech—not anything. In fact, he would have taken even odds that he would be hanged before sundown.

Dressed again and with his hair wet, he felt awake and very alert to danger. He moved over to his fishing lines and was unhappy to see that two were empty and the third had nothing but the head of a fish biting on his hook. Muskrats or beaver had eaten his catch, maybe even a fox or a raccoon. Damn them.

Zack dug around in the damp earth until he found

worms, and then quickly rebaited his hooks, knowing that any fish he caught would likely also be eaten by an opportunistic critter. He did not have time to hike back to the soddie and return with traps, so the furry poacher of his lines would probably get a free Sunday supper.

Zack hurried back across the wheat fields. If a hundred mounted cowboys had boiled over a hill and opened fire on him, he would not have a been a bit surprised. He could still see that cowboy's hate-filled eyes and hear his terrible threat. Maybe they were waiting to hang him and Pa in Cheyenne in front of all the people. That was probably it. They wanted to make it a show. Maybe even charge admission and sell . . . stop it! he told himself angrily. That kind of thinking won't help anything.

Zack made it across the bare fields, and just before he entered their soddie, he climbed up around the hill and stood on the roof. No cowboys in sight. With empty fear in his belly and the rehearsed speech already forgotten, he scurried back down into the yard and went inside, wanting nothing more than to make it to Monday.

The streets of Cheyenne were nearly empty at nine o'clock in the morning. Pa skirted the downtown and came in on the side streets. He was packing his old Navy Colt revolver, but he had not allowed Zack to bring their hunting rifle.

Mother's eyes were brimming with tears. "If you get killed," she said, addressing both Zack and Adolph, "it'll kill me, too."

Pa wiped a sheen of nervous sweat from his cheeks and slapped his whip at the mule. "We won't get killed, I told you!"

They were late, but the congregation was waiting for them and there had been trouble already. Paul Renke had been stopped on the street and cowboys had insulted him while he was escorting his family to church. Darrell Smith was challenged to a fistfight by a huge, drunken Bar 5 hand who had whipped him soundly. And while still lying in the dirt, Darrell had been made to apologize for being a sodbuster and a sorry excuse for a human being. There were other incidents, nothing terrible, but the sodbusters and their families huddled in their small church and tongues clacked nervously until the Reverend Angus Holbert started them singing "Rock of Ages."

Zack had to admire the Reverend's excellent choice of hymns. Even as they sang, he could feel the steadying effect of the hymn on the nervous congregation. When the hymn was finished, they sat down and Reverend Holbert delivered a sermon about how the Israelites had suffered for so many years in the desert and how the Christians had been sacrificed to the lions in Rome. But when the Reverend saw how upset the sacrificing thing was to some of the women and children, he reverted to his main theme which was how no power on earth could overcome God-fearing men and women who refused to sway from the path of righteousness—no matter how terrible the persecution and how many might fall. There would be a Hereafter in which all things would be made right. The main thing was to avoid, at all costs, adopting the violent and sinful ways of the enemy. He talked for a long time about the rewards of Paradise, and when it was over, the congregation looked at each other a little more hopefully than they had when they had walked in the front door.

Carrie thought the entire sermon was nonsense. She believed in God, but not a God who wanted people to turn into lambs and be sacrificed by anyone stronger. Jesus had gotten angry sometimes and he had used a scourge to chase the money changers out of the temple. If there was any fault at all among Christian peoples, it was that they sometimes kept thinking about love while people kicked their heads inside out. *Do unto others as they do unto you*—that was the way Carrie felt about it. If someone hurt you badly, you took an eye for an eye. Carrie glanced at her father who had nodded his pointed chin with every one of the Reverend's exclamations. The hypocrite! You would never catch Adolph Bennett turning *his* other cheek!

The schoolteacher, Miss Newby, got up and came to the front of the church. She was a thin, nervous spinster in her late forties who loved teaching. Only Carrie had guessed that she despised the uneducated, mainly unwashed parents of her precious students.

"Brethren," Miss Newby said, her voice trilling like the song of an excited bird, "children of God. I want to announce again that our graduation ceremony is being held today at one o'clock. Mr. Zachariah Bennett is our honor student and will be valedictorian."

She beamed at him and Zack shifted uncomfortably on the hard wooden bench. His shoes were too small and his feet ached. His suit was thirty years old, the same one Pa had worn when he married Ma. It fit like a feed sack.

"As some of you will remember, Miss Carrie Bennett was our valedictorian last year and her speech was memorable."

Carrie smiled, knowing that she was the only one who

39

remembered that the theme of her speech had been self-determination. But she had coated it with so many layers of words that only the brightest people in the audience could have understood the true meaning. Zack and Ma had understood, yet it was most likely they had forgotten all about it.

"Zachariah, will you please stand up and tell the congregation the theme on which you have chosen to speak at our graduation ceremony? I'm sure it will convince everyone to attend."

Zack unfolded from his seat. Carrie leaned forward expectantly.

"Self-determination, Miss Newby."

"Oh."

Carrie blinked with surprise. That was all Miss Newby had said. Just "Oh."

With an effort, Miss Newby managed to smile, but her voice sounded a bit pinched with annoyance. "How very nice, Zachariah. I'm sure it will be every bit as relevant today as it was last year when Carrie gave it."

Carrie studied her lap and fought down the giggles. By God, Miss Newby *had* remembered! Carrie waited until the teacher was seated again before she took a deep breath and thought, never mind her. It's a good theme and one worth repeating. Maybe Pa will even listen and learn something this time around. When she gave it last year, he had fallen asleep in his chair.

When the service ended, everyone waited to see who would step outside first. Unlike most Sunday mornings, they remained as solidly planted as if their coats and dresses had been nailed to the pews. My Lord, Carrie thought, they think there might actually be cowboys waiting outside to gun us down.

40

"Zack," she said, "let's lead the flock."

He understood. Ignoring Ma's pleading eyes, they walked out, side by side. There were no cowboys waiting to drill them in their tracks, just two drunks asleep down the street beside the livery barn. Carrie expelled a deep breath and then the congregation came outside to stand blinking in the bright sunlight. After a few minutes, everyone began to drift toward the shade of the cottonwood trees just as if it were any other Sunday in Cheyenne.

Zack felt the eyes of the men upon him and his father. He didn't want to talk about what had happened, and when Annie Norton called his name, he hurried to check on their mule. He bent and inspected Jim's hoof as if there was something very important inside of it, and just when he thought that he had given Annie the dodge, she peeked under the mule and said, "Is it true you broke a cowboy's nose with those big, knobby fists of yours, Zachariah Bennett?"

Annie's father raised chickens and sold their eggs as well. Annie was roundish and still chubby-cheeked with her baby fat. Her sunbleached hair was always mussed and her bright blue eyes usually looked as if she was up to something. With her two buck teeth, she reminded Zack of a cottontail bunny. Strangers fussed over her, saying she was cute, but what they didn't know was that Annie had a razor-sharp tongue. She was two years younger than Zack, but almost as far back as he could remember, Annie had been his main rival in the classroom.

"I asked you a question, Zack!" She said it so loud that people nearby stopped talking and watched them.

Zack wished he could run and hide. Instead, he

41

dropped Jim's hoof and straightened. "Who told you that?"

"Dozens of people."

"People with flappin' tongues and big ears, I reckon."

"People with more sense than to go around hurting cowboys! Don't you and your Pa realize we could all get in trouble!"

"I'm sorry," he said, not feeling sorry at all. He hadn't thought about the rest of the sodbuster families being in danger. Especially the Nortons, whom he had never liked. They were whining, tightfisted and nasty people who made a hefty second income by buying out failing sodbusters for less than ten cents on the dollar. They profited from the misfortunes of others. If Annie ever pushed him too hard, he was going to remind her of that fact.

"Sorry won't do much good if they hang any of us sodbusters!" Annie huffed.

"They won't do that."

"Maybe so and maybe not. But if I were you or your Pa, I'd sure be worried."

Zack saw his mother's hand flutter to her mouth and her face lose what little color it had. He turned back to Annie, wishing he could upend her and whip her fat butt. "Get out of here," he growled. "Not having to see and argue with you every day at school is the best part about graduating!"

"I hope they break *your* nose," Annie shrieked, exploding into tears. "And here's this dumb old present I bought for your graduation. I really hate you, Zack Bennett!"

She threw a small, brightly wrapped package at him,

and before he could think of anything to say, she whirled and ran off crying.

Zack looked around, aware that people were staring at him. He studied the crumpled present between his two big feet. Oh, hell, he thought miserably. For a moment, he considered leaving the package and walking away.

"You might as well pick it up and open it," Carrie whispered. "Everyone saw you make a fool of yourself already."

Zack bent and picked up the crumpled package. He tore it open and discovered a beautiful yellow bandanna, the kind the cowboys wore. For a moment, he stood there feeling a lump build in his throat. He was mighty glad that Annie wasn't around to see how much he liked the gift.

"She understands you better than I thought," Carrie said. "Smart girl."

"Yeah." He refolded the bandanna in its paper and stuffed it into his coat pocket. It would not do for his father to see the gift. Pa might know it was the kind worn by cowboys. "I better go practice my speech," he said quietly.

"You need any help?"

"No."

Carrie nodded. She watched her brother walk away and then she went to stand by her mother. The woman was still pale and that scared Carrie. But it would scare her ten times worse on the day that Ma could not climb out of her sickbed and come to church because, when that happened, Ma would be dying. Coming to church and listening to the sermon, then meeting the other women parishioners was her single pleasure. Ma needs to live right here in Cheyenne so she could see and talk to other women every day. If she lived in town, Carrie thought, I could finally run away and she would be all right.

Carrie looked down the street toward the saloons. She heard the faint tinkle of piano music and then a woman's coarse laughter. Carrie had a powerful urge to go visit Cheyenne's red light district, not because she wanted to become friends with a whore, but because she knew that no woman was born bad. Every newborn child was as innocent as Jesus. Carrie figured it might do more good to understand what had gone wrong with sinful women than to assail them for their weaknesses. But, of course, if Pa should ever catch her talking to one, he would horsewhip her almost to death, same as he would if a traveling medicine man or drummer walked her out in the moonlight.

Carrie knew she was old enough to take a man. But there was not a sodbuster in Wyoming, Kansas, Nebraska or Colorado she cared to meet. No sir! And there was no chance to meet town boys who generally looked down on poor dirt-farm girls anyway, and if they paid any notice to them at all, it was only because they just wanted them for pleasure. Farm boys had often tried to talk to her, but she had greeted them with such cold silence that, after a few embarrassments, they had all given up on her. That was fine. Carrie hated the dank, heavy smell of dirt. She awoke in the morning with dirt from their ceiling in her face and she went to bed at night feeling dirt between her toes and her legs. You could hang muslin or cheese-cloth under the rafters of a sod ceiling until it looked like clouds piled to heaven, but the dirt came through and fell on you anyway. It dropped on the food. Fleas and bedbugs bred in dirt. Pa had finally put in a wood floor, but that did not stop the mice, gophers and snakes from burrowing through the earthen walls. And when it rained hard, no matter that the ceiling might be three or four feet thick with alternating layers of sod and brush, it still leaked.

Carrie dreamed of a wood house, or even better, one made of brick, one where you did not feel the heaviness of the grave pushing down on you day and night until you thought you would suffocate. A house that stood right up above ground and did not apologize to earth or sky, one that caught the afternoon breeze in summertime and the warmth of a high plains Indian summer.

Even Cheyenne whores lived above the ground.

No, Carrie thought, gazing up the Sunday morning boardwalks of downtown Cheyenne, if I marry, it will be to a prosperous merchant or—God help me if Pa knew my thoughts—to a successful young cattleman. Not an ordinary cowboy, but a man of some property and growing importance, one who could help her erase the awful Wyoming sod from her mind and her body forever.

"Carrie?"

She snapped out of her reverie and turned back from the street to see Zack waiting anxiously.

"What?"

"It's time to go to the schoolhouse and I plumb forgot the speech I memorized last night!"

He looked so fretful that, instead of feeling exasperated at him for needlessly keeping her up half the night, Carrie took his arm and said, "When a man believes he is going to die before daylight, it's no wonder he forgets his speech. It doesn't matter. You'll do just as well telling them whatever else you are thinking."

"I don't know about that. I sort of remember parts of it. I guess maybe if the cowboys don't shoot me, Miss Newby will."

That remark set them both to laughing as they went to join Ma and Pa and the people who were walking toward the schoolhouse. Carrie wished she could tell Zack about how she intended to marry well. And if that meant a rancher who would also hire her brother and make *his* dreams of being a cowboy come true, so much the better. But right now, there wasn't time to talk. Besides, she could tell by his face that his mind was locked onto the problem of giving a speech that he had mostly forgotten.

It'll probably be more interesting this way anyhow, Carrie thought happily.

Chapter Three

When the smattering of introductory applause had died, Zack laced his fingers together so tightly that his knuckles showed little points of red at the top and the rest of his thick fingers were white.

"Self-determination . . ." he began slowly, ". . . self-determination is important to all of us because this is a land of opportunity and only people with—with gumption and self-determination will succeed—with the help of God, of course."

"Amen, son," Adolph said from his front-row seat. He looked pleased so far.

"Self-determination is what brought our pilgrim fathers here on the *Mayflower*, and even before them, Christopher Columbus. None of those folks left Europe without taking a chance and doing what they figured they had to do. Everyone in Cheyenne has self-determination or they'd have stayed back East where it was safer.''

It did not hurt to flatter folks a little. Zack unlocked his fingers and shoved his hands in his back pockets so they'd be out of his way.

''I believe that freedom to do what a person feels he needs to do is more important than life itself.''

Zack saw Carrie's eyebrows shoot up, but he pushed on anyway. ''And it doesn't make any difference where you come from, because the only thing that counts is where you're going. I believe the good Lord has given everybody something to do and they only need to listen to His word to find out what it is.''

Zack took a deep breath. So far, he had trod easy. He could stick to the safe road and please both Ma and Pa by talking more about God's will, but that wasn't going to make it any easier later on when he set off to satisfy his own ambitions. Best get it out right now. At least, Pa could not very well blow up in front of everyone.

''The hard part in life comes when people want us to spend our lives doing something that we don't much want to do. I believe that self-determination, and the laws of nature, are telling us to be true to God, our country, our families . . . and maybe most of all, to ourselves.''

Good, Carrie thought proudly! She sure hadn't given Zack that line. Pa looked wide awake. Carrie bet his pupils were starting to get small, the way they did when he began to lose his temper.

''Miss Newby is a fine example of self-determination. She came West five years ago and persuaded the town fathers to build a school, and thanks to her, I can read and write, something most grown men cannot do.''

Adolph stomped his foot down hard. He cleared his throat vigorously.

"But that's no shortcoming for a man with self-determination," Zack added quickly, aware of his gaff. "Even the uneducated among us can walk upright in the path of the Lord if he was taught right from wrong."

Adolph's shoulders lowered a little. Zack saw Carrie shake her head and knew she was trying to tell him to move on.

"I guess without self-determination my Pa would have quit homesteading long ago. The railroads in Kansas cheated us Bennetts out of everything, but Pa never gave up. He always wanted to be a farmer and he is still trying . . . to be one. I mean . . . a good one." Zack saw his father turn white with anger. "I meant my Pa is . . ."

"Shut up and sit down, Zachariah!" Adolph roared as he stomped outside. "Your speech is over."

A moment before, Zack had seen a lot of tight smiles in the audience as he had dug himself deeper and deeper into a hole with his big, loose mouth. But now, as his Pa got up and stomped out of the schoolhouse, there were none. Not even from Annie Norton.

Zack tried desperately to think of something to save his botched speech. "I guess," he stammered, "my Pa showed self-determination when he stormed out of here. A lesser man might have sat still and watched his son make an even bigger fool of himself, but not my Pa. He's smarter than that. Thank you."

He bowed from the waist as Miss Newby had taught him and everyone applauded. But they were showing him the same kindness they would a simpleton. He had spoken pitifully.

Ma put her arms around him. Several people came up

and patted him on the shoulder and said nice things, but Zack didn't hear them. He had wanted his Pa to listen this time, but Zack knew his own fool tongue had betrayed him once again. Not that a speech was likely to have changed anything. Pa would still hate cowboys and ranchers, rich men and braggarts, but . . .

"You did just fine, son," Ma said. "Your Pa liked what you said in the first half of your talk. I could tell that. Later on, he'll remember that you mentioned the Lord."

She patted him and then followed his father outside. Some of the women brought out cakes and cookies, milk and lemonade.

Carrie looked at her brother and felt real pride in him, a kind of pride that was a little different from anything she had felt before. He had attempted to put his deepest feelings into words, in front of all those people. So what if it hadn't been an unqualified success. Her little brother was mighty close to being a man.

"Carrie, may I speak to you for a moment, outside?"

She looked to see Miss Newby staring at her, white-lipped with anger. "Yes, ma'am."

When they were alone beside the back door, Miss Newby said, "I guess you put your brother up to that?"

Carrie's chin shot up defiantly. She knew Miss Newby had every right to be furious because she *had* put the ideas into Zack's head that had turned his graduation speech into a disaster. Carrie wanted to cry with frustration. She managed to say, "He was trying to tell Pa something!"

"I guess he did that," Miss Newby said coldly. "He told his father that he is a poor farmer and an uneducated fool. It was cruel to remind him of those shortcomings in front of his friends and neighbors. You should be ashamed of yourself. You are smart, the brightest pupil I've ever taught, but I am beginning to think that your intelligence is also your curse.''

Carrie started to open her mouth to defend herself. But she had never seen Miss Newby so angry, and when she tried to speak, she discovered that she had not the will to utter a single word in her own behalf. Tears filled her eyes and she whirled and ran with her skirts flying.

She hated skinny, mean old Miss Newby and she hated Cheyenne, hated sodbusters and hated her father. All she wanted to do was run away!

She was running out into the middle of the broad main street of Cheyenne. She angrily scrubbed at her eyes and proceeded blindly toward the row of shops on the other side. She was in the center of the street when she heard the thundering hooves of a team of horses behind her. She twisted around and her blood ran cold. There was no driver on the wagon! Carrie found herself rooted to her limbs and she frantically began to retrace her steps. She heard a shout and saw a man spur his horse forward.

''Grab my arm!'' he yelled.

Carrie had an image of a cowboy riding low in the saddle, hatless, with black hair and dark eyes. Their hands slapped together but she missed her grip. His fingers dug into her wrist and then she felt herself being catapulted into the air. Carrie yelped in pain as she slammed into the side of the cowboy's racing horse. She bounced off and crashed into a hitching post and lost consciousness.

When she awoke, she looked up and recognized Dr. Rankin, the cattleman's doctor. Dr. Holstetter treated the sodbusters and he didn't live nearly so well.

51

"Well, young lady," Rankin said, "you were very nearly killed out there in the street. You are a very fortunate young woman. If Mr. Alder had not been riding into town and seen that runaway, I doubt you would be alive right now."

Carrie nodded. She did not need to be reminded how close she had come to death. She looked down at her legs, remembering how those of the cowboy had been crushed last night by their own wagon.

The doctor seemed to read her thoughts. "No," he said, "except for a knot on the back of your head, a few bruises and one arm jerked halfway out of its socket, I'd say you are as good as new."

"Thank you, sir."

"You're too old to race across the street like a schoolgirl. Two people have been killed by runaways this year—but at least they had the excuse of being drunk."

"I wasn't drunk." Where was she? The room was beautiful.

"Of course you weren't. Aren't you the daughter of that sodbuster, Adolph Bennett?" There was strong disapproval in his voice.

"Yes."

"I'll bill him for my services." The doctor stood up and looked down at her faded homespun dress. "But I doubt I'll ever see a cent of my fee."

"You'll see every penny of it!" Carrie said angrily. She tried to rise but a stabbing pain almost blinded her and she fell back on the bed.

"I'll pay her fee, Doc. And also for any medicine the young lady needs. It was a cowboy who got drunk and fell off his wagon. I kind of feel that makes us to blame."

She was astonished to realize that she had been totally unaware of the presence of another man in the room. She turned her head to see the same cowboy who had pulled her out of the path of the runaway team.

"But Rio . . ."

"How much I owe you?"

The doctor seemed to swallow whatever he had been about to say. "Five dollars, including this bottle of medicine I want her to take every morning and night."

"Take my money and go along."

"You'd better let her go with me, Mr. Alder. Her father has a reputation of being a violent man."

Rio Alder was not impressed. He shook his head. "She can't be moved yet. You're the doctor. Look at what happened when she tried to sit up just a minute ago."

"Yes, but . . ."

"I'll bring her along as soon as she is up to being moved. Make sure you leave the door wide open. I wouldn't want to see this pretty young lady . . . ah . . . compromised in any way."

Carrie had not supposed that any man could order Dr. Rankin about that way, but this one did. And when the doctor walked out and she turned to look at him again, she saw that he was standing beside her bed and looking down at her with such a compassionate expression that she immediately felt much better.

"I think I'll feel strong enough to leave in just a minute," she said, studying him closely. He was beautiful; curly black hair, slender, square-jawed. And he had nice eyes. He was well dressed, too, with a bandanna just like Zack's, only it was red. He wore a mustache and long sideburns. He looked absolutely dashing.

Carrie's fingers smoothed her dress. Her face was probably smeared with dirt. He must think her exceedingly common. Had it not been the Sabbath, he would have seen dirt in all the creases of her skin.

Carrie's eyes flicked to an oil painting on the wall. It had a gilded frame and the wall itself was covered with a lovely sprigged paper. A crystal chandelier hung overhead and the bed she lay on was incredibly soft.

"I've never seen such a nice room. It's beautiful." It smelled nice, too, but she would not show her lack of good manners by telling him what he must already know.

He smiled and glanced around. "Sort of extravagant, but after sleeping on the ground all the way up from Texas, I figured I had it coming." He looked back down at her. "The doctor said you are a sodbuster's daughter. I guess maybe you aren't used to fancy hotels."

She shook her head. He was staring at her so intently that she looked away. "Which hotel am I in?" She had seen them all from the outside.

"The Cattleman's."

It was the finest in Cheyenne. "I really don't belong here," she said, her mouth feeling a little dry. "I better go."

"Wait," he said quietly. "You're so darned pretty I want to look at you just a while longer."

Carrie felt her heart leap. Shamelessly, she asked, "Do you really think so? I mean, that I'm pretty?"

"I'd be willing to wager that you are the prettiest girl in Wyoming," he said with a smile that made Carrie feel as if her very bones were turning to mush. "Dr. Rankin told me your name is Miss Carrie Bennett."

"That's true."

He removed his hat and bowed. Like most men of the saddle, he wore a Stetson so habitually that when it was removed there was a band of white forehead below his hairline that the sun never touched. He stuck out his hand and said, "It's an honor to make the acquaintance of such a beautiful lady as yourself, Miss Bennett. I consider myself a lucky man to have saved your life."

Carrie felt as if she could die and go to heaven because—in her whole life—things could not get any nicer than this. "You got the words to take a woman's breath away, Mr. Alder."

"Rio," he said. "My name is Rio Alder. My father is Jefferson Davis Alder of Prosperity, Texas."

She wished he were from Cheyenne. "What brings you to Wyoming?"

"Cattle. Me and my boys delivered a herd to a rancher here but he went broke. We're sending the herd east on the Union Pacific after they rest and fatten up a little."

"I'm sorry to hear that. I hope you did not have to settle for a poor price."

Rio shrugged as if it were of no great importance. "The livestock buyer gave us a fair shake. I telegraphed my father and he okayed the sale terms. Six thousand dollars is worth driving them north for, Miss Bennett. Even all the way to Cheyenne."

Six thousand dollars! Carrie could not imagine that much money, not if she tried for a hundred years. Rio and his father must be rich men.

"I once knew a girl almost as pretty as you are," Rio said. "I kissed her. I was only thirteen and she was twelve."

Carrie blushed. "What happened afterwards?"

"Nothin'. We were just kids. How old are you?"

"I am . . . nineteen." It was a bald lie and it popped out without conscious thought.

He chuckled. "No, you are not. I'd guess you're more like seventeen."

She flushed with embarrassment, for he had pegged her exactly. "How old are you?"

"Twenty-one." He suddenly sat down on the edge of the bed.

"I'd better go," she said. Carrie glanced at the door. It was wide open.

He touched her cheek. "I guess a kiss for saving your life would be too much for this plug-ugly Texas cowboy to expect."

"You're not ugly, Mr. Alder. You're anything *but* ugly. But if . . ."

When his lips came down and covered hers, Carrie forgot whatever it was she had meant to say. She didn't even try to resist because she owed Rio Alder her very life. She let him wrap his arms around her and kiss her so passionately that she almost swooned. He didn't want to stop and she didn't want to stop. But she did.

"Please," she whispered, "I don't think I should let you kiss me like that."

"You've never even been kissed, have you?"

It was not really a question and she knew better than to be caught in another lie.

"No."

He smiled. "Well, I'll be! Down in Texas, a girl as pretty as you would have to beat cowboys off with a stick. The men up here in this country must be blind or mighty timid."

"Nothing timid about you, is there?"

"Nope." He bent to kiss her again. "And if you let me close that door for a little while, I'll show you a whole new world, Carrie."

She had neither the will nor the strength to push him away before he kissed her once more. It seemed as though she had been dreaming of being held by a man like this all her life, one handsome and good, kind and sweet-talking. Carrie felt as if she were lost in a dream—a dream she knew would end all too soon. The thought of returning to their homestead and the soddie filled her with quiet desperation and she clung to Rio Alder tightly.

But then, she heard a strangled cry from the hallway and Rio's lips were tearing away from her own. Rio was wearing a gun, and as he reached for it, the strangled cry became a terrible roar as her father rushed through the door.

"Pa, no!"

Adolph had grabbed a shovel somewhere along the street and now he brought it crashing down on Rio's shoulder. The Texan's six-gun flew out of his hand and Rio was knocked spinning halfway across the room. "I was only kissing her for . . ."

Again the shovel whistled. It caught the overhead chandelier. Glass shattered and Carrie ducked. She heard a grunt of pain and looked up again to see Pa smash Rio in the chest. The blow sent the young Texan crashing through the window to disappear into the street below.

"You've killed him!"

But Pa was insane with anger and he wanted to make sure Rio was dead. He spun around, threw himself into the hallway and then raced down the stairs. Carrie could hear his thudding footsteps hit the lobby floor. Seconds

57

later, as she dizzily stumbled into the hallway herself, she heard shouts from the street below.

By the time she reached the street, she found Rio dazed and bloodied, yet very much alive, thanks to a gang of cowboys who had knocked her father down and were now beating him senseless.

Carrie flew to Rio's side. "They're going to kill him!" she begged. "Stop them! Please."

Rio managed to get to his feet, and when he looked at Carrie and saw her panic, he staggered over to a cowboy, yanked out his six-gun and emptied it into the sky.

The gunfire had the desired effect. The cowboys piled off Adolph, but they hadn't wanted to. Carrie dropped down beside her father. Zack and some of the other sodbusters came racing up the street from the school yard.

For a moment, Carrie thought that the cowboys were going to shoot every one of the farmers.

"Hold it!" Rio Alder shouted. "I got one more bullet in this gun and the first man who moves gets it!"

The two factions halted and then Zack detached himself from the sodbusters and hurried to his father. He signaled to the homesteaders. "Help me carry my pa over to Doc Holstetter's office. Hurry up!"

They started to come forward, but the cowboys blocked their path. One of them said, "That's the same crazy old sonofabitch that ran over Art yesterday and crippled him! I say we bust his legs and even the score."

"And *I* say this is finished!" Rio shouted. He pointed the gun at the knot of vengeful cowboys.

Zack stared at the young cowboy, amazed that one of them would turn on the others. But then, it took only one glance to tell him that this man with the Texas drawl was different from any he'd seen. Rio wasn't quite as tall as he was, but he seemed ten feet high right now. He was covered with blood and wicked-looking shards of glass. His curly black hair was down in his face and there was a nasty cut on one cheek. Even the fist that held the six-gun was bleeding. The Texan's savage appearance stood everybody up in their boots.

Zack grabbed his father under the arms while two others took a leg apiece. Zack glanced at the man with the gun. He was in awe of him. "I won't forget what you just did for my pa."

Rio nodded. He turned to Carrie. "You better run along with your own kind."

But she hesitated. Everyone was looking at her. She didn't care. This young rancher had saved her life and now he was cut and bleeding. "I . . . I'll meet you at the doctor's in a few minutes," she whispered. He would know that she meant Dr. Rankin.

Rio pitched the six-gun back to its owner. The aftermath of a beating which had left Adolph Bennett unconscious was just now having its effect on the faces of the cowboys. There would be no more violence this day.

Rio looked at her closely, "Are you sure?"

"I *have* to see you again," Carrie whispered, leaning close as she reached up and touched his glass-torn cheek. "Rio, you saved my life and then . . . then this is the thanks you receive."

He nodded and said softly, "You can make it up to me later."

Her cheeks burned scarlet. "I will." She touched his face, knowing she was acting crazy. It was all insane and even impossible . . . because rich, handsome men weren't supposed to take an interest in the daughter of a dirt farmer. Rio Alder was far too above her, but Carrie could not change the way she felt. For the first time in her life, she understood the meaning of love, and how a woman listened to her heart, not her head.

"Carrie!" Zack shouted, "come along with us!"

She raced after them. Her mother would need comforting. But the moment things settled down, she was going to Rio's side.

"Bring him in here, quickly!" Dr. Holstetter said, leading them into his office and gesturing toward a table. "Put him right there and then I want everyone outside but family."

Carrie stepped back. She watched the doctor strip her father of his shirt. She had not seen her father's bare torso in years. At night, he was never without a shirt, for he considered the bare chest of a man as immodest as that of a woman. Carrie was shocked at how thin her father was; she could count every rib.

"Who did this?" the doctor asked tightly.

Zack and Carrie looked at Ma, but she seemed dazed by this sudden misfortune. "Is he going to live?" she whispered.

"I don't know yet, Mrs. Bennett. Your husband has a pulse, but it's weak and too fast. His breathing sounds wet in the lungs, but I don't think a rib punctured one. His color is fair."

The doctor peeled up Adolph's eyelids and studied them closely, then turned his head with about as much reverence as a man would turn a watermelon and then thump it for ripeness. Dr. Holstetter examined both of Pa's ears. Carrie saw blood in the right one.

"I think he has a severe concussion. Yes, quite definitely."

"Will he die then?"

"Not likely, Mrs. Bennett. But he can't be moved and he might not wake up for days. Even if he were conscious right now, I would say he could not be moved for a week or two."

"But we got no money to stay in town!"

"Move him too soon, he'll suffer brain damage and die."

Ma didn't seem to be listening. She was distracted and confused. "We got livestock that got to be tended. Acres of weedin' yet to do and . . ."

"Ma," Zack said quietly. "Me and Carrie can do those things. You stay here with Pa."

She looked at him and he saw that her eyes were wet with tears. "We ain't got the money to stay, Zack! And Mr. Slater won't give us the oxen if Pa don't finish that sod work. We *need* them oxen. You remember what happened to the wheat last year."

"I remember. I can do all the sod laying by myself. I helped with our soddie, remember?"

Carrie placed her arm around her mother's thin shoulders. "I'll do the weeding and care for the livestock. Zack can finish the work for Elmer Slater. Everything will get done."

"But . . . the money."

"Mrs. Bennett," Dr. Holstetter said, looking at her with professional concern. "There's a shack out behind my office. I keep it furnished for just such a reason as this. You can stay there for free until it is safe for your husband to travel. Your children are grown. They can bring you bedding and food. It shouldn't cost you any more to stay here in town than it would at your homestead."

She frowned, a little suspicious and trying to see the dangers. "But we ain't paid you yet for the last time you came."

"You can pay me when you harvest your wheat next fall," he reasoned to her slowly, patiently. "And if you want, you can clean up the house and the office, do some mending and things for me in trade. I haven't had much help since my wife died. This place is in a fix."

Now Zack saw his ma finally relax. Housecleaning, mending, these were things she could do to help. She was not a woman who could be happy being beholden to anyone for long. It was surprising, since she had never known a single day when she had five dollars to her name.

"I *could* do that," she said hopefully.

"Sure you could. Now, why don't you go rest in the shack a while, Mrs. Bennett. You look exhausted by the trials you have just suffered. I think the rest here might be the best thing that could have happened to you."

"I ain't important. It's Carrie and Zack, them's the ones that's important. Adolph would say the same if he could speak."

The doctor looked at Carrie. "Why don't you take your mother out and make her rest easy? There is nothing better for your father right now than to sleep."

Carrie nodded and led her mother through the back door. The shack was small but much nicer than their soddie. The wooden building had a sturdy potbellied stove, a table, bed and plenty of nails in the walls to hang your clothes on. In a soddie, you couldn't drive nails in the walls because they'd just work themselves out in a few days. And no potbellied stove ever made could eat away the chill of the grave.

Carrie put her mother to bed and she fell asleep within five minutes. She hurried out and almost ran into Zack.

"How is she?"

"Scared, but so tired she went right to sleep."

Zack shoved his hands deep into his pockets. "Those men would have killed him if that one hadn't stopped them. Who is he?"

"His name is Rio Alder. He's from Prosperity, Texas, and he and his pa own a big cattle ranch."

"You know a lot about him."

"He saved my life, and then Pa's. I thought it right to know something about him."

"What happened in the hotel?"

She told him everything except that they had kissed. By the time she was finished, Zack's face had darkened with anger. "You shouldn't have gone to his room!"

Carrie shouted, "I was out cold, you idiot!" She was sick and tired of defending herself to Bennett men. Even Zack.

Her outburst shocked him and brought him up short. She was right to be angry. It had not been an hour since she had almost been run over and killed. If it had not been for Pa, everyone would still be remembering the runaway wagon and feeling hollow in the belly.

Zack drew a deep breath. "I'm sorry, Carrie. It's just that everything has gone so foul today."

Carrie made herself smile. "Look," she said, the anger washing out of her, "last night, on the hill, we both thought that the cowboys would come and shoot the bunch of us. You said you did not expect to live until morning. Remember?"

"Yeah." Last night was a hundred years ago.

"Well, we *are* alive. And maybe Pa's getting beat up so bad will end the trouble."

"I don't believe that."

Carrie didn't either, but she managed to say, "Well, maybe it will."

Zack nodded without enthusiasm. "I better go on back to the homestead. Why don't you spend the night here and watch Ma. She's pretty upset. I'll come back for you in a day or two."

"You sure?"

"Yeah. If I leave right now, I can still get a couple of hours of weeding in before dark."

"All right."

Zack left her then. Carrie gave him five long minutes. And then, instead of turning around and going into the shack, she combed her hair with her fingers and hurried down the alley behind the doctor's office. She was going to see Rio Alder.

She might never have another chance like this in her whole life.

Chapter Four

Zack had hoed weeds by the light of the moon until long after midnight, until he could not keep his eyelids open and the hoe in his clenched fists seemed as if it were made of stone. He did not eat before collapsing into bed because it was sleep he needed, and yet, it was his curse that deep exhaustion brought insomnia. He struggled to sleep, but the harder he struggled, the more impossible it became to turn off the thoughts that whirled around and around in his mind.

So much had happened so quickly in his normally dull life! In less than two days, everything had changed for him and Carrie. Last night, the whole family had been together at supper and then he and Carrie had studied his graduation speech before falling to sleep on the burying hill. Zack had expected to be attacked by the cowboys and taken, along with Pa, to some distant tree or telegraph pole and hanged. But tonight there was real hope. Maybe now that the cowboys had whipped Pa, they'd be satisfied and life would return to normal. But then again, maybe it wouldn't.

Until just a few days ago, Zack had believed that his life might be just as hard and disappointing as his Pa's. True, he and Carrie had dreamed of better things, Carrie of a life in an above-ground house with lots of sunlight and he of becoming a cowboy. But those had been just dreams. Nothing more. And deep in his heart, Zack knew that no rancher would hire a sodbuster. Why should he? There were plenty of experienced cowboys looking for work who could already ride and rope and do a whole lot more than milk a cow, weed a wheat field and build a poor soddie.

But that was before Rio Alder. The Texan had changed everything when he had saved Carrie's life, then Pa's, not an hour later. Rio had spawned within Zack a bold and desperate plan of escape. Maybe the plan was crazy, but maybe not. If Rio helped his pa and his sister, maybe he'd even help him become a cowboy. Or at least tell him how an ignorant man goes about getting work on a cattle ranch. There must be chores that the real cowboys didn't want to do and so a rancher might gladly hire a greenhorn like himself. Just give him a start mending things around his ranch house or digging wells. Zack had heard it said that cowboys did not like to work on their feet. Well, he reasoned, that's the only kind of work I know.

It all hinged on whether or not Rio would take pity on him. Shoot, stranger things in this world had happened, hadn't they? And Zack took some comfort in knowing that now he at least had a cowboy's yellow bandanna. So, when he went to ask Rio for a job, the Texan might see that bandanna as a tangible sign that he was sincere in his desire to better himself.

The thing that had Zack most worried was that the Texan and his cattle-driving crew might have already headed down the long trail south. And the next most worrisome thing was the idea of leaving Carrie and his Ma behind while he sallied forth to bold adventures in Texas. Just thinking about abandoning Carrie and Ma to this poor dirt farm filled Zack with guilt and set him to wondering if he could do it and hold his head up like a man. But . . . but dang it! It just seemed likely that, maybe, God . . . yes, God had sent Rio Alder to save Ma and Carrie and then himself from this miserable Wyoming homestead.

And wouldn't it be something to come back next spring all gussied up like a cowboy with three or four months of wages in his pocket to give to his pa and ma? Maybe if he did that, then it would be all right. Pa might finally see that it wasn't the clothes a man wore or whether he made his living following a plow or a cow that mattered. He was still the same person and there were good cowboys, the same as there were good farmers. People were people every time, if you could get past the trappings.

Zack hung onto that thought through the wee hours of the morning. The image of himself riding up with his yellow bandanna, cowboy boots instead of old broken work boots with low or no heels, a Stetson and Levi's instead of bib overalls filled him with such pleasure that he ceased to worry about sleep.

And because of that, he finally did sleep.

*   *   *

Red Rooster woke him up just after sunrise. Zack rolled to his feet and crawled back into his bib overalls. He staggered over to the water barrel and drank deeply, then took a second dipper outside and poured it over his head. The cold water did little to revive him this morning. His eyes burned and he ached with weariness. Zack walked back inside the soddie and started a fire. While the stove heated, he cut a few more potatoes and whittled at a three-pound chunk of salt pork he had purchased at Ned's Meat Market in Cheyenne. The pork had cost him six bits, but even Pa would have to say that a man can't weed and build a sod house on nothing but a diet of potatoes, cornmeal and sourdough.

He went out and milked the cow, and when he came back inside, the stove was crackling and ready. Zack fried up the pork and the potatoes and drank a half gallon of the warm, creamy milk. He began to feel better.

The sun was a head high off the ground when he finally got the oxen yoked and the wagon hitched. Without a backward glance, he headed up the Lodgepole Creek road toward Elmer Slater's place. He sure wished that he could finish up Elmer's sod work and help Carrie with the weeding before Pa came home from Cheyenne. But most of all, Zack wished he could dig a well deep enough to find water. That would be a proud thing to do, and if Rio agreed to take him along to Texas, Pa wouldn't be able to say anything against him about leaving Wyoming with work left to be done.

"You are damn late!" Elmer Slater swore, stepping out of his soddie. "Where is Adolph?"

Zack climbed down from the wagon. He knew that working near Slater was going to be a trial, but it was one he was determined to pass through without discrediting himself.

"Pa's in Cheyenne," Zack said. "He got beat up by a passel of cowboys. Carrie almost got run over, but one of them saved her and then later Pa, too."

"What the hell are you talking about, boy!"

Zack began to unhitch the wagon and then rehitch the grasshopper plow. He explained to Slater in more detail, and when he was finished, the man said, "You mean a Texas cattleman stood up against his own kind for your Pa?"

"Yes, sir."

"Then he wants something."

Zack thought that was ridiculous. The Texan sure hadn't stopped to figure out the risks and advantages of helping either Carrie or Pa. "Heck," he said, "we don't have nothing he would want. Cowboys don't need our mule and they don't drink milk, so the cow is no good to 'em. We don't have but a few dollars of money and I wasn't even wearing the new bandanna that Miss Annie Norton gave me as a present."

"Humph!"

"Well," Zack said, trying not to get riled so early in the day. "I wasn't! And that bandanna is the only thing that a cowboy would want from us."

"You sure?" Elmer Slater had a shrewd and a distrustful mind. "Maybe he wants to diddle around with your sister. Carrie's a damned good-looking little filly. Plenty of spirit, too."

Zack stiffened. If Elmer had said that to Pa, the fat man would already be on his back with a boot filling his dirty mouth.

Zack turned slowly to face the man. "Mr. Slater, you

say any more about Carrie and I'll whip the living daylights outa you, so help me God.''

Slater flushed. ''You can't talk that way to me!''

''I just did. But you danged sure can't talk that way about Carrie.''

Their eyes dueled for supremacy and when Zack broke the man's gaze, it gave him no satisfaction at all. Elmer Slater was a low sort, even if he did have a new windmill and a bunch of nice things. Having nice stuff did not make a fool wise, nor a weak man strong.

''You hear about that widow, Henrietta Locke, dying over in the next county?''

''Nope,'' Zack said, hitching the plow.

''Well, she did and her son wants me to come over this morning and make an offer on their butter churn and some of the things the widow owned. I guess I will, but I don't trust leaving a kid here to do a man's work.''

Zack bristled. ''Go or stay, it don't matter because you can look over what I done when you come back and see for yourself it's just as you asked.''

Elmer nodded. ''Oh, I'll do that for sure, boy. And I expect some real progress to be made while I'm gone. Don't you be hanging around and trying to wheedle food outa the Missus.''

Zack grabbed his father's whip and laid it smartly across the backs of the oxen. He did not trust himself to speak to the man. He drove the oxen over to the patch of bare earth and tipped the plow upright. ''Gee up, thar!'' he shouted, cracking the whip right in their ears. ''Move, ox!''

The lumbering beasts threw their shoulders to the task and the silver blade cut into the hard, black soil.

Zack plowed for almost an hour, and when he looked

again at the Slater sod house, all he saw was some kids, the Slaters' old hound and a lot of waving grass. Elmer had taken his own wagon and gone to see the widow Henrietta Locke's son to beat him out of his mother's treasures for a pittance.

Zack worked through the morning without halting to rest. After a quick meal of pork and some bread, Mrs. Slater brought him out a slice of rhubarb pie which he ate with great enjoyment. Then he went back to work, plowing, loading the rectangular hunks of sod and then driving back to the house and packing them two-thick, interlaced, the way that Pa had taught him. Like most sod houses built with any real thought, Mr. Slater's soddie was situated foursquare to the points of the compass. It was a sign that a man knew direction and order. Not having a compass was no excuse for a house to be laid out all catty-wampus. Zack had watched his own Pa set a stake and then tie a rope to it and line it up with the North Star, giving him a line that was true north and south. Then Pa had simply made a square and used more rope to lay down the other three sides to their new house.

In this case, Zack's only real challenge would be to build a good roof. Most sodbusters set a tightly packed layer of willows or marsh grass over the rafters and beams before adding a layer of hard clay and then one of sod. They were hoping to keep the roof waterproof, but willows and hardened clay still leaked badly in a really heavy rain. Now Slater, being a man of some wealth, had bought lumber from an old wooden barn near Cheyenne. He'd dismantled the barn and hauled the wood over to be used as the ceiling, walls and floor. What he was doing, Zack figured, was getting himself an underground cabin built. It would be mighty nice and almost certainly waterproof; Zack knew it would be the envy of every sodbuster family for miles around.

By late afternoon, Zack was worn out, and when he saw a cloud of dust on the horizon, he guessed it was Elmer coming back to criticize his work. But he was wrong. It was Bob Lumen and he came racing right up to the soddie as if something was wrong. Lumen was a man in his late forties, a neighbor of theirs.

"Zack," Bob hollered, even before he had come to a complete stop. "Do you know what that sister of yours is up to!"

Zack didn't like the man's tone. "She's older than me. I reckon what she does is her own business."

"Well, when your Pa gets off his sickbed, he sure won't take it the same way. That girl is taking up with Rio Alder in the most shameful way. She's even keeping company with him!"

Zack lunged forward and dragged Bob right out of the saddle. It was no great feat. Bob was smallish and thin. He was also too loose with his tongue.

"You want to tell me what you just said once more," Zack asked, his hand knotted into a big fist.

"Well," the man said, his eyes scared like those of a caught rabbit, "I was only saying that everyone in town is saying! And I saw her with my own eyes. She was walking down the center of town with that damned Texan just as big as you please. Laughing and having a high old time of it while you're out here working yourself to death and your Pa is halfways beat to a pulp. It just isn't like Carrie. She's a fine girl and raised right, too!"

Zack shoved him away. "You actually saw her with him?"

"Yep!"

"Walking arm in arm?"

"And laughing like there wasn't a brain between the two of them."

Zack scowled and turned away, his mind awhirl. It was natural for Carrie to be grateful to the man for saving her life, but it wasn't natural for her to traipsing all over Cheyenne with him.

"That there fella is a ladies' man, mark my words, Zack. He'll turn Carrie's head and lead her astray."

That was what Elmer Slater had said in his own smutty little way. The memory of it brought Zack's anger to a fresh boil. "Well," he said hotly, "I reckon that Carrie just might turn the Texan's head some, too. And there's nothing wrong with a girl her age sparking with a young cowboy."

Bob Lumen stared at him as if he had not heard correctly. "You addled from hard work or something, Zack? Don't you know that Adolph will kill that Texan just for *looking* at his daughter? I'd say he left you in charge of things, but you're doing a mighty lax job of it."

"I got to finish this soddie in order to get the oxen!"

"Are even a dozen oxen worth the virtue and name of a good woman gone bad? I tell you, I seen them strollin' along together like they was man and wife. It ain't right, and the loss of her reputation is going to be a hard burden for your folks to bear when they hear about this."

"And I don't have to ask who will tell them, do I?" Zack said harshly.

"The whole town saw them, not just me!"

"Ride on outa here, Bob. Leave me be awhile to think on this."

"You better get to Cheyenne before nightfall," Bob warned. "That's all I got to say. After that . . . well, no matter what Carrie might do, she'd be judged guilty if she ain't already."

It was true. Zack had heard the farmers and their wives gossiping a time or two. They could be especially hard on one of their kind who strayed from the path of righteousness.

"Ride on, Bob!" The sharp prod of worry had already replaced the anger in Zack.

The man spurred his horse into a gallop. He had a soddie over near Buffalo Wallow, and except for Sundays at church, you never saw him or his wife and their eight children.

Zack tried to go back to work. He was about done laying the sod he had cut and worry about Carrie made him hurry to finish up and be gone. He worked with fresh zeal and then he hitched the oxen back to their wagon, leaving the grasshopper plow right in the field where it lay. Elmer would get mad that he didn't bring it up to the house, but Zack did not care. Sundown was just a few hours away and he had to find Carrie and get her out of Cheyenne before she ruined her life.

He rode Jim bareback into Cheyenne, pushing the old, lop-eared mule as hard as it would travel. Normally, Zack would rather be shot than seen riding Jim, for there was nothing more typical than a sodbuster bouncing along astride a big-eared mule without even the comfort of a saddle. Even with worrying about Carrie, he was still self-conscious enough not to put on his bandanna until he could leave the mule somewhere and go find Carrie.

The light was dying when he tied Jim in front of the doctor's office. He hesitated, trying to decide whether or not to go inside and see to his ma and pa first or go hunting Carrie.

In the end, he decided that he had best go in and visit, in case Carrie had come to her senses and belatedly joined them.

"Zack?" his mother asked when he opened the door. "What are you doing in town at this hour of the night?"

His eyes quickly scanned the room. No Carrie. "I . . . ah . . . I was just worried about you is all."

"We are fine. Pa woke up today for a while and he seems a lot better. But he's already gone to sleep again. He didn't say much. Just picked at his food."

Zack looked across the tiny room at the still figure of Pa and tried to form the question that plagued his mind. "Carrie," he stuttered, "I was . . ."

"You shouldn't have left her all alone out there, Zack. Did she get to weeding early this morning?"

Zack's heart almost broke. In misery, he realized that both Elmer Slater and Bob Lumen had been right about the Texan. The man had undoubtedly ruined poor Carrie, dragging her into the everlasting fires of hell and damnation.

"Zack! What's wrong with you? You been workin' way too hard again, ain't you?" She was not a tall woman and hardship had worn her down until she just looked used up, but she still had it in her to wither a man with a disapproving look. "I always said you and your pa was too much alike. He worked himself down

75

to nothing but skin and bone and a nasty temper. You're only sixteen and you're doing the same.''

''There's a lot of work to do out there, Ma,'' he answered, trying to collect his shattered thoughts.

She leaned in close to him and her fingers reached up to smooth the skin of his cheek. ''The work will keep a day, Zack. Your pa could never sit still a minute when there was something to do. He'll kill himself in the fields one day. I know that. It's like he was trying to atone for all that we lost in Kansas. But he can't. That don't matter to me anymore. You and Carrie are what matters now. Promise me you'll take tomorrow and rest. Just care for the livestock and don't do nothing else.''

''I can't,'' he said. ''Mr. Slater wants me to finish up that soddie, and the weeds just keep growing bigger. Either we take care of things or Pa will come home and try to catch up all at once and kill himself for sure. You don't want that, do you?''

She shook her head. ''This land is gonna kill both of you, Zack. It ain't no good for farming. I know that and so does your pa. But he's stubborn just like you. Neither of you is a quitter. I *am* proud of that. But I still wish you'd take tomorrow off.''

He kissed her good-bye, saying, ''I better get on back now.'' He turned toward the door and then hesitated. ''Ma?''

''Yeah?''

''You look better than you did yesterday. You look more rested than I've seen you in a long time.'' It was true. One full day's rest and she seemed to have dropped five years.

She actually smiled. ''Cheyenne agrees with me. I

went out awhile today and I talked with some ladies. I did!''

"About what?" Zack could not imagine what his mother would have to talk about with any town women.

"About lots of things, including how to make a good sourdough starter. Anyway, you hurry on. Say hello to Carrie for me. Tell her that we are fine.''

"I will," he promised.

She gave him a quick peck on the cheek and then she shoved him out the door.

Zack headed straight for the Cattleman's Hotel because, if Rio Alder was still in town, that's where he would be staying. He tied his new bandanna around his neck and strode along the boardwalk, acutely conscious of his bib overalls and the fact that he was barefooted. But that was not important, not at all, compared to the trouble he had facing him about Carrie and Rio Alder being together.

And how could you challenge and fight a man who had saved the lives of both your pa and your sister?

The Cattleman's Hotel had always been off-limits to sodbusters and farmers. Its lobby was the pride of Cheyenne. It was cavernous in its dimensions and huge chandeliers hung from the ceiling, their lights blazing off an immense hardwood floor, bare except for a few Navajo and Hopi rugs. The lobby was ringed, ten feet above the floor, with the heads and horns of dozens of trophy animals. And over the massive fireplace hung the enormous head of a Texas longhorn steer.

Along the eastern wall there was a hundred-foot-long bar backed by a beveled glass mirror that was framed in gold. Along the western wall stood the hotel desk behind which clerks waited at rigid attention, ready to assist a well-heeled patron at the snap of a finger.

The Cattleman's Hotel was more elegant than anything between San Francisco and St. Louis, even the upstart Denver to the south had nothing to compare. And while the hotel's almost sixty rooms were occupied primarily by cattlemen, railroad officials and other dignitaries who passed through on their way from one coast to the other were frequent guests. The elegant hotel was also a favorite gathering place for wealthy foreigners who had come to see the West. At any time of day, a man could hear at least three languages being spoken in the lobby and saloon areas. Zack knew that common cowboys were allowed to mosey inside the Cattleman's, but they would be served only one drink before they were asked to leave. Drunkenness and profanity were not tolerated, no matter what the status of the individual. And if a cowboy became belligerent or if his appearance was rough, he would be escorted forcibly out the back door.

Zack had seen that happen. Like many of the sodbusters' children, he had spent more than a few secret hours outside the Cattleman's, peering through its imported stained-glass windows. The stiff clerk would eventually drive them off, but not before they had had a chance to glimpse a world they had not known existed.

Now Zack stood outside the front door of the Cattleman's Hotel, summoning up his courage. He would rather have walked into a snake pit than cross the twenty feet to the hotel desk. He took a deep breath, tied his yellow bandanna around his throat and pulled his pants legs down as far as they would go.

Zack had not covered half the distance across the

beautiful polished floor before the desk clerk spotted him. The man's eyes widened as if he could not believe what he saw. Zack heard all conversation die and the huge lobby became so quiet that the only sound remaining in his ears was the tight squeaking of the soles of his bare feet on the wood. He finally made it to the desk and faced a man who wore a uniform and a badge that labeled him the Desk Captain. The man was looking at him as if he were an insect.

"What are you doing in here?" the man hissed.

"I came to see Mr. Rio Alder," Zack said, feeling the eyes of every man in the room boring into him. "It's important."

"What could you possibly want with Mr. Alder that could not wait until after he had departed these premises?"

"It's about my sister," Zack said in a very low voice. "I think she is with him right now and I've come for her."

The Desk Captain blinked. He had been about to summon a couple of burly escorts, but now he paused. "What is the . . . uh . . . lady's first name?"

"Carrie. She has blond hair and stands about this tall." Zack showed the man. "Is she here?" He could not help himself; he glanced up the staircase toward the rooms above.

The Desk Captain frowned. "No," he clipped, "we do not allow single women to visit the rooms of our guests. And as you can plainly see, the woman is not in the salon. Now, scurry out of here before I have you tossed out."

Zack gripped the edge of the desk. "Well, has she been here?"

"Please, lower your voice." The man leaned forward conspiratorially. "Yes, she was here only a few minutes ago, with Mr. Alder. I believe they went out for dinner. Now, I have told you all that I will, and you must go before I have you thrown out."

"That's fair enough," Zack said, realizing that he had been flanked by two husky hotel employees. "I thank you for your information."

The Desk Captain made a rapid sweeping motion with his long, smooth fingers, as if he were brushing a piece of offending lint off his sleeve. "Go-o-o," he said, drawing the word out and turning away, "quickly."

"Where might they go for dinner?"

The two men grabbed him by the arms and their grips were so strong that it never entered Zack's head to struggle. They practically lifted him off the floor and carried him outside where he was thrown off the veranda to land by the seat of his pants in the dirt.

Zack got up and brushed off the dirt. He stared up at the pair and they stared back down at him. "Just go," the biggest one said in a kind voice. "We don't like to hurt little farm boys."

Zack left.

It took him less than a half hour to find Rio Alder and his sister. They were seated at a secluded table in the fancy El Rancho Steak House. He had been kicked out of three restaurants and now there was an anger in Zack so strong that, when a waiter tried to stop his advance, he flung the man aside and marched right down the aisle to where Carrie and Rio were sitting.

"I think it's time you came home," Zack said, reaching for her.

Carrie had been smiling radiantly, but now her smile died and she recoiled from him as if he were a snake. "No," she said, "I'm not going back there!"

"Won't you sit down," Rio said, almost as casually as if they were about to discuss the weather. He snapped his fingers. "Waiter, bring us another bottle of wine and a tall glass of whiskey for this man. And cook him up a Delmonico steak like the one I ordered. Put plenty of onions on it."

Zack had no idea what a "Delmonico" steak was and he had never drunk wine or whiskey. He had no intention of doing so now. "I got to take her home," he said stubbornly, "but first, I need to ask where she stayed last night."

Rio's easy smile died on his lips. He was dressed in a tailored black coat, white shirt and string tie. A fine black Stetson was resting on its crown beside him. For some reason, Zack noticed that the hat was lined with white silk clean enough to read the name of the maker, J. B. Barney and Sons, Cheyenne, Wyoming.

Rio sighed and drawled, "Miss Carrie stayed all night at Mrs. Radley's Boarding House for Ladies. Would you like to excuse yourself and go check that out?"

Zack touched his sister's arm. "Is that true?"

"Yes." She turned to look at him and her eyes were as hard and shiny as glass beads under water. "But I don't suppose you'll believe that, will you? You've got all the makings to turn out just like Pa. Just give you a few more years and you'll be spouting the Bible."

Her hot, accusing words stung him deeply. Zack bowed his head and stared at his big, work-roughened hands. He felt awful.

The waiter came. "Here," the Texan said quietly.

"Best whiskey money can buy. Toss it down neat and it'll relax you so we can talk."

Zack stared at the glass of whiskey, then he squared his shoulders and drank it in one gulp. It was like drinking liquid fire and big tears squeezed into his eyes and he choked, feeling as if his protesting stomach were a volcano about to erupt.

"Drink some of this burgundy wine," Rio said, his lips forming an amused smile as he handed him a crystal goblet. "First swallow always goes down the hardest. After that, you might even start to think you like it."

Zack drank the entire glass, and though it still did not quell the burning sensation that ran from his belly to the base of his tongue, it did help. After the whiskey, wine seemed like water. Zack wiped his eyes with the back of his hand. He rose and shook his head. When he tried to speak, he discovered his voice had taken on a gravelly sound and he had to clear his throat several times before he could spit out his words.

"I got to take you home, Carrie. People are already talking about you and Rio. You know what'll happen when Pa hears the talk."

"I'm not going back home. Look at me, Zack! Look very close."

He scrubbed his eyes again and stared at her in the flickering light of the candles.

"Do you see the difference?" she asked.

Anyone not blind could have seen the real difference. Carrie's hair was fixed up prettily on the top of her head in a way that made her look downright royal and about five years older. She wore a new satin dress, either soft blue or gray, he could not be sure in the candlelight. She was also wearing perfume that Zack found so powerful as to be disconcerting. She looked scrubbed and as shiny as a new penny. Just sitting across the table looking at her, a stranger would never have guessed in a hundred years that she was a poor sodbuster's daughter. Even something in her expression was different. She seemed . . . somehow irreversibly changed.

"Carrie," he admitted, "you turned beautiful."

His answer seemed to catch her off balance. She had been ready to attack him with cutting words, but now she dissolved into tears.

"Well, Goddamn!" Rio swore with exasperation. "This is some party we're having, just the three of us! Maybe we ought to just shoot ourselves and be done with so much fun."

Carrie sniffled. She dabbed at her eyes with a lacy silk handkerchief. She forced a smile and held up her glass for Rio to fill.

"Let's have a toast!" she ordered. "To life and to adventure! To escape from soddies and to never look back."

Rio filled all their glasses. The scab on his cheek was the only flaw that Zack could see in the man and it reminded him of how his Pa had knocked Rio through the second-story window of the Cattleman's Hotel only two days ago.

They were waiting for him to join them in the toast. Zack obliged. He clinked his glass to theirs and then he drank deeply. The wine was dry as powder and it had a strong taste that filled his nostrils, but it did not choke or burn like the whiskey.

"That's the way," Rio said, clapping him on the shoulder and filling their glasses again. "This is French wine and it ought to be sipped. But, tonight, I think we should just forget about 'ought to be's' and think only about good things. Zack, Carrie tells me you want to be a cowboy. Is that right?''

He was taken off balance. What else had Carrie told this man? But all he said was, ''Yes, sir.''

Rio grinned. ''Good! I heard you gave that old milk cow of yours quite a bucking out earlier this spring.''

Zack flushed with embarrassment and did not trust himself to answer.

''Did you know there is going to be a rodeo this Saturday, just south of town?''

''Nope.''

''Well, there is,'' Rio said. ''I'm riding in it and so are some of the boys. It'll be sort of interesting, Texas against Wyoming cowboys. Carrie will be there. Why don't you come along and join the fun. Everyone will have a good time. If I don't get bucked off first time out and land square on my head, I'll give you a few pointers. How would you like that?''

''There is nothing I'd rather do,'' he said quite simply. ''But I can't. I got a soddie to finish for Mr. Slater, a well to be dug, and about three acres of weeding to be done before Ma and Pa come home.''

''It will be longer before Pa comes home than we first thought,'' Carrie said. ''I talked to the doctor and he said Pa isn't doing as well as he had hoped.''

''But I talked to Ma less than two hours ago and she said . . .''

Carrie cut him off. ''I *know* what she said, but I talked to the doctor. Pa is weak and he's fainted a couple of times when he tried to get up and walk. The doctor says that he must have gotten booted in the head. He'll be all right for a few hours, then keel over.''

Zack discovered his hand was shaking when he reached for the wine. He drank it fast. "How long will that go on?"

"The doctor doesn't know yet. Two weeks. A month." She shook her head and clenched her hands tightly together. "A year! There's just no way to tell. He won't be able to go back to prove up, Zack. It's all finished."

The enormity of what she was saying hit Zack like a speeding train. Homestead law said you had to live and prove up on your land for five uninterrupted years. It also said you had to raise and harvest crops and dig a well which produced water. This, the fourth year, was the one they were to have dug the well. But now . . . if Pa did not recover.

Carrie had always been able to read his mind. "That damned homestead doesn't matter, anyway," she said angrily. "Zack, can't you see how it was killing us! Look at me and Ma. See how being back among people and things has made us alive again. Can't you see how it is?"

"But that's our land. It's our home!"

"Our home? Don't you remember how we always dreamed of escaping? Was it all talk for you? Just big talk of being a cowboy and roping cattle and all that?"

He shook his head. It was one thing to go off and be a cowboy, but quite another to let four years of back-busting toil go for nothing.

"Zack?"

He looked at Rio and the Texan said, "There are some things we need to talk about. First, Carrie and I are going to be married and live on our ranch in Texas."

Zack's jaw dropped.

85

"And, second, I want you to come down and live with us. I'll teach you to be a cowboy."

He could scarcely believe what he was hearing. It was as if all of his dreams had come true. And yet . . .

Carrie saw the doubts rise up in her brother's eyes. "This is our chance!" she whispered fervently. "Zack, you don't owe them any more of your life. Come with us! Please."

He wiped his face and reached for the water. It rippled in the glass in his hand and he drank it quickly. "Whew," he managed to say, "you sure move fast, Rio."

"I love Carrie," he said simply, "and that's why we're having a big wedding down in Texas. But Texas is a long ways away. It'd kill my family if I was to marry up here in Wyoming. So the marrying will have to wait. But we couldn't, Zack. Do you understand what I am saying?"

When the realization of what Rio meant hit him, Zack felt his cheeks burn and he could not look at his sister. "When are you leaving for Texas?" he managed to ask.

"About a week. We want you to come with us."

"Where are you . . . I mean, what . . ." He could not find the words to ask the question that needed to be asked.

"We'll be staying at the Antelope Hotel," Carrie said. "We'll be living there until we go."

Zack looked up at her with misery in his eyes. "It'd be a whole lot easier on Ma and Pa if you just said good-bye and went."

Rio shook his head. "I wish we could do that, but we got to wait until the money for those cattle comes and that won't be until next week."

"Then Carrie should stay with me at the soddie," he said stubbornly.

Rio shrugged, letting him know that such a decision was up to Carrie.

Zack looked at his sister. "Well," he asked, praying that she would agree.

"We just told you what happens here doesn't matter anymore. It's done. I'm staying with Rio."

Zack knew he had lost. "Then I'm going home," he said, pushing to his feet. "I got to get an early start tomorrow. There's a lot to be done."

"Leave it!" Carrie's voice was high and strained. "Just leave that damned hundred and sixty acres of prairie. Let it go!"

He shook his head. "I don't guess I can rightly do that. Not until Pa is well enough to come take it. It's just not mine to leave, Carrie. It belongs to all of us."

"Well, you can keep my part of it!" she cried.

Rio took hold of Zack's arm. "I want you to come with us and be a cowboy," he said. "You haven't seen or done anything in your life yet. You've been yoked like your oxen. It's time to break free and have some fun. You don't want to be nothing but a sodbuster all your life."

Zack stood there, caught in the web of indecision. "I guess I got to think on it some," he finally said.

"What about your steak?"

"I just lost my appetite," Zack replied, feeling a little ill and still unable to look directly into his sister's eyes. "And I'm going home."

Chapter Five

In the days that followed, Zack did not quite feel that anything was real. The news of Carrie and Rio's impending marriage in Texas, on top of the disturbing report on his father from the doctor, was too much change all at once. Zack thought about Carrie and his parents during his every waking hour and also about Rio's unbelievable offer to teach him cowboying. But even though he should have been deliriously happy—he was not. Maybe, he reasoned, it was because, up until the last time he had talked to Carrie and Rio, he had always supposed that *he* would choose the time of his leaving the homestead. Thinking about escape had been a comfort of sorts, a thing with which he could gently drift along whenever the reality of homesteading and being dirt-poor seemed intolerable.

But now, Carrie was really leaving—with or without

him. Pa was sick, the weeds were growing so fast he could barely keep up with them and the well needed to be dug. How could he leave at a time like this? And yet, how could he not. He'd never again have such an opportunity and he constantly reminded himself of the theme of his graduation speech, self-determination, of doing what it was you wanted to do, instead of spending your life trying to live up to someone else's expectations.

Zack was torn from within, a man divided. With so much burdening his mind, physical work was a comfort and he drove himself hard. He awoke before dawn each morning and then weeded for an hour after daybreak before going in to eat. After that, he yoked the oxen and drove them over to Elmer Slater's where he labored until long after dark.

On Friday, he finished by the light of the moon. His sod-laying had been first rate; even Elmer seemed pleased, though the man tried to get him to come back and set the doors and windows in their wooden casings.

"No, sir," Zack said, his resolve firm. "I heard my pa make the deal and we was to do all the sod work, but not the carpentry. If I was to accidently break a window, you'd charge me for it and I have no money to pay so you'd lay claim back on the oxen."

He shook his head and stamped the ground barefooted in anger. "We had a deal and it is done."

Mr. Slater argued vehemently, but when he finally saw that Zack would not give in, he relented. "I don't think you are a good enough man with hammer and nails to do the windows and door right anyway," he groused.

"You're right on that one, Elmer." He had never

called the man by his first name before, but it now seemed natural. Man to man.

Elmer stuck out his chubby hand and they shook. "Zack," he said, "you did good work. You can work for me anytime. A dollar a day and found."

"No, thanks."

Zack took the fine yoke of oxen as his own. He left Elmer and his family, though he was sorry to say good-bye to Mrs. Slater and the children. Without consciously realizing it, he had come to enjoy their company.

That night, he took his pa's smoking pipe and walked up on the burying hill. He filled the pipe and lit a match to it. The first lungful of smoke made him cough until his eyes stung and tears streamed down his cheeks. He roughly put the pipe aside. Smoking was a nuisance, a luxury and a habit that he could not afford.

Zack watched the stars, knowing the hour was growing late and he should go to bed. But, as usual, he was physically exhausted and yet there were too many thoughts in his mind to sleep. What was Carrie doing right now? Was she enjoying one of those fancy Delmonico steaks and more wine? Or was she already in Rio's arms in a bed? Zack shook the thought from his mind because it was too painful to consider. He had always been taught that the physical union between a man and a woman was fornication unless they were married. Carrie had been taught the same, but she obviously had either forgotten or did not believe it—and Carrie was a whole lot smarter than he was.

Tomorrow was the rodeo and he had decided to go and watch. Maybe he would even ride a horse or something. Then he brought himself up short, thinking with disgust, wouldn't I look fine in my bib overalls and my bare feet? They'd all laugh themselves to death and the horse would be too ashamed to buck.

Zack picked up his father's pipe and shuffled down the hill toward the soddie. He saw big clouds floating across the face of the moon and they looked promising. Maybe there would be rain tonight or tomorrow. He hoped so. A good, warm rain would save the wheat and allow the sodbusters to invest another year of their lives. Come on, Lord, he thought, bring us some rain!

It did rain all the next day and Zack had no time to go to the rodeo to watch Rio and the Texans, even if they were crazy enough to try to rodeo in a thunderstorm. Instead, he hoed in the mud until it was nearly dark and he was shivering so badly that he had to go inside, light a fire and change into dry clothes. Later, he put on Pa's heavy overcoat and work boots and fed the livestock, taking special care to check on the oxen. And after that, he fell asleep in front of the fire, so tired he could not even summon up a dream to carry him through the stormy night.

It was still raining early Sunday morning when he hitched up Jim and headed for Cheyenne. There was a strong, cold wind coming down from the north and it pushed the rain sideways, making it come down in a wavy sheet. Sometimes, ice pellets struck the earth and scattered like rice. But they melted almost as fast as they came. Pa's overcoat quickly soaked through and water sluiced off his old felt hat. Zack felt hot, then cold. He had to grind his teeth together to stop their chattering. The mule was balky and ill-tempered. It walked down the muddy road like a fastidious cat and its long U-shaped hooves made sucking sounds. Zack rode all the way to Cheyenne in the rainstorm, wondering, each time he came to a low place between the hills and saw the heavy runoff of water slicing away the soil, if perhaps the downpour was going to do more harm than good. He frowned, knowing that the small wheat plants could wash away or simply drown if the ground became saturated. Zack watched bolts of lightning stab out of the clouds which formed a dark, undulating lid of gray. The prairie grass surged in the wind, as wet and angry-looking as a storm-tossed ocean.

Twice, the lightning struck the hills nearby and Jim almost managed to wheel around and race back to their farm. But they finally reached Cheyenne and Zack drove straight up the sloppy streets to the Antelope Hotel, where he was determined to see Carrie and have a talk with her about Rio. He had hit on a simple solution that would satisfy everyone; they could get married twice, once here by a simple justice of the peace, and then they could have a big church wedding down in Texas. It would save a lot of heartaches. That way, nobody could shame Ma and Pa by telling them that their daughter had lived openly in sin.

The Antelope was a cowboy's hotel and Zack could feel antagonism the moment he opened the door and scraped the mud off the soles of his boots. There were no more than a dozen hands, but they had the look of dissipation and resentment about them. They were probably cowboys who had squandered their wages on Cheyenne's Saturday night delights, intending to head on back to the ranches on Sunday. But the storm had changed their plans. Men who rode the prairies did not ignore lightning storms. Too many of them had seen their companions fried.

Zack pulled off his floppy hat and whacked it against

his leg a couple of times. Then he squished across the room in his Pa's big work boots.

"I want to see Rio Alder," he said to the man behind the front desk.

"He already checked out." The desk clerk looked at Zack with scorn. "Who are you?"

"Zachariah Bennett."

"The girl's kid brother?"

Zack heard a low rumble of snickers from the cowboys who were listening without pretense.

"Miss Carrie is my sister," he said, knowing his face was reddening. "Where did she and Mr. Alder go?"

"Rio went back to Texas," the man said. "Your sister, she just stayed in his bed."

The lobby exploded with cruel laughter. Zack felt his insides go cold. "He left her?"

"Yep," the man said, starting to play to his audience, "though I'm sure the reason she hasn't crawled out of their room is that Rio told her some cock-and-bull story about him coming back someday. But, hell, why would a cattleman like that bother to come back for a two-bit, whoring . . ."

Zack swung with every intention of smashing the leering desk clerk's face in. His bony knuckles connected solidly and the man crashed into the wall. Zack went over the top of the desk and hit him again. The man screamed and Zack drove his fist into the desk clerk's lying mouth, feeling teeth break under his knuckles. Lobby chairs scraped as cowboys flew to the man's rescue.

Something exploded against the back of his head and he staggered. He turned to fight and three men piled on him, bearing him down to the floor and raining punches.

They pinned his arms under their knees and beat his face until it was numb and he lost consciousness.

He awoke choking to death on what he thought was his own blood, but it was the runoff from a gutter feeding down onto his face. Zack rolled over in the mud to rest on his stomach. He lay still for a long while and then pushed himself erect, grabbing onto a rough wall for support. He was in the alley behind the Antelope Hotel. He staggered, slipped in the mud and fell. It was easier to get up the second time, and slowly, his mind sized up the circumstances as he remembered why he was in town.

Carrie.

Zack looked up at the rear of the Antelope Hotel. There was a staircase, probably built to accommodate a whore's customers rather than serve as a protection of life during fires. He staggered to the stairs and began to climb. There were only fifteen steps, but it seemed as if he had climbed a mountain before he reached the second-story landing.

Thankfully, the door was unlocked and he stumbled in out of the rain to stand dripping in the hallway. There were eight doors on the landing, four on each side. The first two were locked, the third one opened and sent him staggering into a whore's room where he saw things he wished he had not, and in the fourth room, he found Carrie.

She was sitting beside the window, still as a statue, staring out at the rain. For a moment, he hardly recognized her because of the dark circles and the devastation in her eyes. Even in a nice dress, she looked terrible, and when he spoke her name, she did not seem to hear him.

"Carrie?" he said again. He moved across the room to her. "What happened?"

She glanced at him. Her expression was distracted, her gaze unfocused. She said, "He's gone, Zack. But he'll come back if something didn't kill him. He promised to come back for me. And I'll wait right here until he does."

Her voice was dead. Between them, the bed was rumpled and he could see the indentations where two heads had rested on the pillows. He avoided looking at it again.

"How long have you been waiting?" he asked gently.

"What day is it?"

"Sunday."

"He left Thursday." She spoke in a monotone. "He was going to meet with a cattle buyer and get paid for his herd, then come back."

She finally turned to look up at him. Her expression was one of utter desolation. "Oh, Zack, I should have gone, too. I'm so afraid that he got killed!" Ignoring the fact that he was muddy and wet, she hugged him very tightly.

Much later, Zack left her in the room after locking the door behind him. He exited by the rear stairs. He was shaking on the outside, burning on the inside, but all the fists that had landed against him did not cause half the pain that seeing Carrie alone in that room had caused.

He went to a water trough and peeled off his Pa's coat and woolen shirt. He shoved them into the trough and the water clouded with mud. Zack used his shirt to sponge his face, neck and arms clean. He dunked the shirt again and wrung it out by twisting it hard. Then, he redressed and headed for the stockyards, to find out if Rio's herd of longhorn cattle had been shipped on the Union Pacific railroad going east.

"Hey!" a stockyard wrangler yelled, galloping his horse down through the gutters of mud that filled the stockyard and created a stench evident for miles. "What the hell are you doing!"

Zack wasn't doing anything. After slogging through a mile of mud, his strength had deserted him before he had been able to navigate his way through the maze of stockyard alleyways to its offices. Now, he sat with his head down between his knees, his body trembling violently. He could not stop shivering and his legs refused to hold his weight.

"Hey, mister! Answer me and get outa that mud!" The cowboy was reluctant to climb off his horse, but finally, when his challenge brought no response, he dismounted and crouched beside Zack. Tipping back the sodbuster's head, he examined the battered face and the bluish skin and said, "Boy, you are a mess for certain. Someone has beat the hell outa you good."

He grabbed Zack under the arms, surprised at both his height and the lightness of his body. He managed to shove Zack across his own saddle and then he led his horse through the mud. He would half ruin his boots and saddle, but he would do no less for a weak calf. He guessed even a sodbuster deserved equal treatment.

"Who is he?" the wrangler's boss said as they carried Zack inside and laid him down beside the stove.

"Don't know. Just a sodbuster I found."

"Better go get the doctor. This boy looks like he's freezing to death. He's shaking so hard his bones are rattling."

"Which doctor?"

GET YOUR 4 FREE BOOKS NOW—
A VALUE BETWEEN $16 AND $20

Mail the Free Book Certificate Today!

FREE BOOKS CERTIFICATE!

YES! I want to subscribe to the Leisure Western Book Club. Please send my 4 FREE BOOKS. Then, each month, I'll receive the four newest Leisure Western Selections to preview FREE for 10 days. If I decide to keep them, I will pay the Special Members Only discounted price of just $3.36 each, a total of $13.44. This saves me between $3 and $6 off the bookstore price. There are no shipping, handling or other charges. There is no minimum number of books I must buy and I may cancel the program at any time. In any case, the 4 FREE BOOKS are mine to keep—at a value of between $17 and $20! Offer valid only in the USA.

Name_____

Address_____

City_____ State_____

Zip_____ Phone_____

Biggest Savings Offer!

For those of you who would like to pay us in advance by check or credit card—we've got an even bigger savings in mind. Interested? Check here. ☐

If under 18, parent or guardian must sign.
Terms, prices and conditions subject to change. Subscription subject to acceptance. Leisure Books reserves the right to reject any order or cancel any subscription.

GET FOUR BOOKS TOTALLY *FREE*—A VALUE BETWEEN $16 AND $20

▼ Tear here and mail your FREE book card today! ▼

PLEASE RUSH
MY FOUR FREE
BOOKS TO ME
RIGHT AWAY!

Leisure Western Book Club
P.O. Box 6613
Edison, NJ 08818-6613

AFFIX
STAMP
HERE

"Get Holstetter. He ain't too particular to work on sodbusters and farm animals." The wrangler's boss straightened up and stared out the window across the feedlot. "Damn," he whispered, "this is sure gonna be a mess for a couple of weeks. Gonna stink up town for sure."

The wrangler nodded without listening. He stared down at the tall, thin body covered with mud and cowshit. Some people came to sorry ends, some before they even had a chance to know better.

The wrangler shook his head sympathetically. He had felt Zack's fevered skin and did not think the young man had a chance of surviving. But that, he decided as he headed for the door, was up to the sodbuster and his doctor.

Dr. Alfred F. Holstetter shook his head and put his stethoscope back into his medical kit. "You're a very sick young man, Zachariah. Very sick. You've got a fever and a touch of pneumonia. I want you to stay off your feet for at least a week and not do any work for a month. We have to get those lungs clear."

He studied the two older people. "Mrs. Bennett, I can see that the rest is doing you wonders. You look ten years younger already. By the time you leave Cheyenne, you'll feel like a new woman."

Pa said, "With Zack laid up, we have to go home today."

"I would strongly advise against that." The doctor snapped his bag shut. "Moving this young man in this kind of weather could be a fatal mistake."

Ma nodded. "Then we won't do it, Doctor. Carrie is

out on the homestead and she can take care of the livestock. That's the important thing.''

The doctor looked at Zack with a question in his eyes.
Zack said nothing. But when Holstetter left a few
minutes later, Zack pushed himself up on his elbows,
knowing that he had to tell them about Carrie. If for no
other reason than that someone had to milk the cow and
feed the stock.

Ma placed a hand on his forehead. "You lay back
down, son, and rest. Everything is going to be fine.''

Zack's head rolled back and forth on his pillow.

"But it ain't, Ma. You see, Carrie isn't out at the
homestead anymore.''

"What!'' Pa was suddenly looming overhead. His jaw
was set, his eyes accusing. "Where is she then!''

"She's right here in Cheyenne. She's waiting to get
married, Pa.''

His mother moaned like a hurt animal, but his father
reached down and gripped his arm tightly. "To who!''

"Mr. Rio Alder, the Texas cattleman you knocked
through the window.'' Zack felt the terrible force of his
father hanging over him like an avenging angel. "Pa,
she *loves* him! They're going to live in Texas!''

"No, Lord. No!'' Ma cried, her hands making little
fists that beat at her breast.

"That harlot!'' Pa screamed, his fingernails biting into
Zack's flesh. "Where is she! Tell me, Zachariah!''

"No!''

"Then I'll find her myself, by God! And when I do,
I'll whip her within an inch of her life until she repents
in the name of Jesus!''

Ma whirled and threw herself at him, begging him to
be merciful, but Pa was insane with fury and nothing

could have stopped him from grabbing his stock whip and bursting outside.

"Oh, sweet Jesus!" Ma wailed. "He'll kill her for sure!"

Zack rolled off the bed. "Get me my clothes." He started coughing so hard that he could not get his breath and almost fainted.

Ma shook her head. "You're too sick, Zacky, the doc said . . ."

"Hurry!"

Ma got his clothes. They were wet and muddy, but he did not care. She helped him get dressed and then to get on his feet. At least ten minutes had passed since Pa had grabbed his whip and bolted out the door. Carrie might already be dead.

"Get me that rifle, Ma."

Her face reflected shock. "Oh no, please, Zack!"

"You said it yourself! He'll probably go crazy and kill her when he finds her up there in that hotel room. It's up to us to stop him, Ma. Nobody else but us can save Carrie now."

Her eyes filled with tears and she sniffled, but she went and brought him the rifle. Together, they barged out of the shack and slogged through the muddy alley to the street.

"This way," Zack said, trying to keep from dropping the rifle. It seemed immensely heavy. "Hurry!"

Carrie had seen her Pa coming, seen the stock whip in his fist and known it was for her. She did not move from the window, not even when he stopped a cowboy who pointed up at her where she sat staring. For a moment, their glances met and Carrie saw a murderous fire in her Pa's eyes. If she locked the door or left the room and managed to hide for a few hours, he would cool down and become rational again. He always did, but Carrie simply did not care about moving. Or hiding. Or even living without Rio.

So she remained seated in the stiff wooden chair beside the grimy window overlooking the muddy street and she waited.

When the door crashed open, she did not even turn.

"Whore!" he screamed. "Promiscuous vessel of Satan! Repent before God, or as He is my witness, I will strip the corrupted flesh from your wicked body!"

A bolt of lightning jittered out of the sky and sparked against a hill just north of Cheyenne. The whip lashed out and it caught her across the shoulders. Carrie bit her tongue and tasted blood. The whip was torn back and it hissed again like a snake. Carrie was knocked off the chair and then yanked to her feet.

"Whore!" he screamed, throwing her toward the hallway. Then he dragged her down the stairwell into the lobby.

The sneers and grins on the faces of the cowboys abruptly changed to expressions of horror. They had never seen a woman beaten with a stock whip. And yet, so great was the fury of Adolph Bennett that they hung back as the girl was hurled out into the street to land sprawling in the mud.

The whip lashed once more and then a rifle shot boomed down the street. Thunder cracked and the rain fell harder.

"No more!" Zack croaked. "No more or so help me, I'll kill you, Pa!"

Adolph turned and advanced, whip up and ready to strike. There was insanity in his eyes. He was crazed with anger. Zack swallowed, tried to pull the trigger. He could not do it. The whip cracked and its tongue bit into his arms and he fell back.

Ma grabbed the rifle from his hands and threw it to her shoulder. "Adolph," she screeched, "drop the whip or by the Lord God I will smite you down!"

The whip was up to strike. Zack saw a hard gust of wind send his Pa's hat skipping a block down the street to settle in the mud. Adolph turned his face to the stormy sky and raised his fist in fury and stood there challenging God Himself. But finally, he turned and plodded down the street until he disappeared around a corner as if carried away by the wind and the rain.

Ma was helping Carrie to her feet and calling for Zack to get their wagon, for they were going home. And that is what they did. Twenty minutes later, Ma was driving the mule with Zack on one side of her and Carrie on the other.

"What about Pa?" he asked.

"He needs to walk home and make his peace with himself and his God for what he done to Carrie back there. It ain't never going to be any good here again. Not with the shame of this on us. I ain't even going to go to church no more. I couldn't face up to them."

Zack was shivering violently. He looked to the sky and all he could see were dark storm clouds on the horizon.

Chapter Six

Their winter wheat had grown waist high and this latest
hole in the earth was twenty feet deep. And still, they
had not found water. This was the third dry hole they
had dug with bucket and shovel and Zack was beginning
to despair if they would ever strike water. Pa had given
up entirely. He spent his days either hoeing in the wheat
field or else off somewhere cutting sod with their oxen
and a grasshopper plow.

Zack climbed out of the deep hole and shaded his
eyes. The late August heat blanketed the plains and the
prairie grass was like straw, dry and almost as golden-
colored as their wheat, only much shorter. Zack liked to
watch their wheat swaying in the afternoon breeze and
he liked to think about how, barring some calamity, the
sodbusters would have a good year and finally make a
living from their toil. He wanted to leave the homestead

knowing his ma and pa had all the improvements made and some money in the bank.

And he *would* leave this time, right after the harvest and after he had finally struck water. A soddie on 160 acres of lonely prairie wasn't much, but it was something, and it was all that Ma and Pa could ever hope to own.

He saw Carrie up on the burying hill, sitting between the graves and staring south. She would be thinking of Rio Alder and wondering why he had not returned for her and if he was dead. Zack wondered, too. At first, he had been inclined to believe that the man had abandoned Carrie after using her for his own lustful pleasure. But then he remembered Rio's courage and how he had saved Carrie and Pa. He had risked his life for them and that kind of a man did not sully a girl's reputation and then leave her to be mocked and ridiculed. Something terrible must have happened to him. But what?

Carrie believed that Rio had been called back to Texas by an emergency and that he wanted her to come to him so that they could be married. But Zack didn't buy that. If the Texas rancher had been forced to go south in a hurry, he still could have taken Carrie with him or at least spent a few minutes letting her know the reason for his disappearance.

Nope, Zack thought, the man is either dead or he deserves to be, for ruining my sister.

Carrie *was* ruined. The fun and the spirit formerly so evident in her every word and gesture had deserted her entirely. She never laughed or even smiled. Her once sharp tongue and even sharper wit were now dulled by despair. She had lost weight, too much weight. Neither food nor sleep refreshed her. She was a shell-woman, an empty vessel that lived and breathed, would answer in monosyllables, but obviously did not care about anything except Rio Alder.

Twice, she had actually tried to walk to Texas. Both times Zack had overtaken her on the plains and found her simply walking along, her eyes drilled on some distant marker to the south. Zack had seen much hardship, but the sight of his frail, expressionless sister shuffling across the vast empty prairie had filled him with inconsolable sadness.

She told him she preferred to leave before the snows of winter if she could, but if not, then she would go even if it was during a snowstorm. Zack knew that she was not bluffing. She would sneak out in a blizzard and walk until she froze to death. For, if she could not have Rio, it was death that she sought.

"After the harvest and the well is dug, I'll take you to Texas and we'll find him together," he had told her.

Only a flicker of her eyes indicated that she had understood—and would hold him to his promise.

Zack wiped his calloused hands on his overalls. There wasn't a cloud in the sky and a hot wind was coming out of the west, making the wheat ripple. Zack judged that it was almost time to harvest the wheat. He would talk to Pa this evening.

Down by Lodgepole Creek, he saw a flock of geese swing up from the marshy grass and circle for altitude. He could hear them calling to each other, rising higher and higher on the hot, lifting air. He saw them line out and head south, and when their squawks died, the prairie grew very hushed. Zack listened intently, hearing neither birds, crickets nor anything but silence.

Zack ducked back into the well hole and slid down

the steeply inclined sides to the bottom. During the past week, he had shoveled his way through layer after layer of clay and loam until now he was down to sand. The sand might hold water. It *must* hold water. He would not leave this homestead and let it go back to the government for lack of a producing well.

He spit into the palms of his hands, gripped the shovel handle and began to dig, putting his hard, whipcord body into each bite of the shovel and thinking how every inch closer to water was bringing him closer to freedom, to helping Carrie.

Hours later, a distant cry interrupted his labored grunts and the grating whisper of the shovel as it sliced into the sand. Zack ignored the cries until they became shrill in his ears. He looked upward to see his mother.

Her eyes were dilated with shock. Her smallish mouth worked silently as she struggled for speech. Zack felt a river of fear rush through his body. The shovel slipped forgotten from his hands. He thought of Carrie, Carrie with the muzzle of Pa's rifle pressed to her temple. "Ma, what's wrong!"

"P-p-prairie fire!" she gulped. "It's comin' fast. We ain't going to be able to outrun it!"

He came out of the hole, tearing away many of his carefully chopped handholds. And the moment his head cleared the earth, he knew his mother was right. The fire was only a mile away and at least ten miles across. Its flames were shooting up to the sun and a huge cloud of black smoke boiled to the heavens and beyond. It was roaring like a freight train and running hard on a wind that would carry it right over the roof of their soddie and across their precious wheat field.

Zack felt momentarily paralyzed with fear. Why

hadn't they seen it sooner! Why, because he was down in that damned hole and Carrie and Ma were in the sod house doing mending, with the doors and windows covered to keep in the morning coolness. And Pa was off somewhere cutting sod.

Zack ran to the corral and opened it. He jumped for the mule's forelock, but the animal was quick with fear. Jim whirled and kicked, narrowly missing him with his hooves. Eyes wild, it bolted through the corral gate and started running. The mule was old and he had never seen it run before. Jim galloped with stiff little hops. Zack watched for a few moments, his eyes judging the speed of the mule against that of the advancing inferno. Jim was already as good as roasted.

He got a rope on the milk cow and dragged it bawling from the corral. "Carrie, open the door!" he shouted.

The door flew open and Carrie grabbed the rope. The cow did not want to go inside. It could feel the heat building and the poisonous smoke was already flowing across the yard. The cow began to thrash its head back and forth and fight the rope.

"Ma!"

She threw herself at the cow and the animal was pushed through the doorway mooing and rolling its eyes like big marbles.

Zack saw Red Rooster flap across the yard and dive into the haystack. Without thought or good sense, Zack ran after the bird, feeling the heat start to burn the hair on his body. He dove into the stack of hay and surprised even himself when he caught Red Rooster by one leg. He yanked the bird out and felt it pecking his bare arm and hysterically beating him with its wings as he raced toward the sod house.

106

Sodbuster

Zack threw the rooster in the doorway and grabbed the outside wash bucket. He sloshed it across the wooden door and window casings, and when he was certain the shirt on his back was going to ignite, he lunged for the door and ran face-up into the back of the cow. It kicked and he hit the wall but did not feel a thing. Carrie slammed the door shut just as the inferno pounced on the roof of their soddie.

Zack grabbed Carrie and his mother and they huddled together under the hillside, back where the earth was damp and cool and where Ma stored apples and potatoes. They heard glass explode. A great *whooshing* sound filled their ears. Zack twisted around to see the cow running blindly around in their soddie, trampling the furniture and bawling in terror until it collapsed and lay panting with its tongue hanging out as big and as swollen as a man's forearm. Carrie hugged Red Rooster to her breast. It was too terrified even to squawk and its round red eyes seemed abnormally large.

But as quickly as it had come, the fire was gone, racing across the prairie on a stiff wind, devouring the grass and every living thing in its path.

Zack stood up. He looked around the soddie and saw destruction. The milk cow came to its feet and shook its head, staring through the window of melted, shattered glass.

There was no grass in the yard right outside their soddie. Zack shoved the smoking door open and it crashed to the earth because the leather hinges which bound it to the door frame were burned away. The cow ran skittishly through the opening into the smoky, pinkish light. The sun was gone. Ash fell like hot snowflakes to cover everything. Little fires danced on a carpet of charred grass. To the east, the flames were like a giant curtain, shivering redly in the distance. Their wheat field was white ash that swirled in the smoke. And Zack saw Jim, a small, smoky black mound.

"Praise the Lord," his Ma said, coming up and taking his hand, "it's over and done."

He turned to her and understood that she did not mean just the fire. Ma wanted to let the homestead go because life out here was too mean.

Zack said, "I wonder if Pa escaped."

Gesturing toward what had been the wheat field, Ma said, "Maybe it's better if he didn't. This might snap his mind altogether."

Carrie came out to stand by them. She was smiling and almost looked happy. "We can finally go now, Ma," she whispered. "It's time for me and Zack to go to Texas."

Zack started to protest. "But we can't . . ."

"You promised me," Carrie said. "I hold you to your promise now. There ain't nothing here to do anymore. It's all gone."

"But what about our Pa! He might be dead."

"I hope he is," Carrie said, just as casually as if she had wished someone a pleasant day.

"Take her, Zacky," his mother said with real urgency. "It's the only chance she's got left."

"But what about you?"

"I'll be fine. Either your Pa will come riding the wagon back and we'll head for town to live, or else one of the neighbors will come along and I'll hitch a ride with them. Go on now. I want to climb the burying hill and say good-bye to your little brothers."

"Are you sure?"

"I'm sure. There ain't nothing to hold any of us here anymore. It's time, Zacky. You can be a cowboy now."

He lifted his hands and started to place them on her thin shoulders, but she turned away and left him to face Carrie and her frozen smile.

An hour later, they were walking south, first across charred prairie, then long after dark across good clean grass. They walked with the north star at their backs and a couple of bundles of food and every extra piece of clothing they owned slung over their shoulders. It was crazy, but it was happening. They were going to walk to Texas and find Rio Alder.

They walked all night and it became obvious even to Zack that Carrie was obsessed with putting distance between them and their homestead as quickly as possible. Or maybe it was just that she was afraid Pa might overtake them.

Zack figured it was probably Pa. Since that terrible day in Cheyenne when he had dragged Carrie out of the Antelope Hotel and publicly proclaimed her a harlot, everything had been a tense and horrible strain, even between Ma and Pa because she had sided with Carrie.

Pa felt betrayed by his family. At every chance, he scalded Carrie with his accusing passages of scripture. Many times Zack had wanted to shout at his pa that God was merciful and that forgiveness was the obligation of all Christians toward all sinners, especially one like Carrie who had acted foolishly, but out of love and misguided faith. Besides, it did not take being God to know that Carrie had suffered too much already.

So, as they walked swiftly south, Zack found himself looking back almost as often as Carrie. And Zack knew that, if Pa should come and try to take them back to the homestead, he would fight. Carrie had only one slim chance left for happiness and he was going to make sure she got it.

Dawn found them crossing a wide creek, and when they joined up with a teamster and hitched a ride toward Denver, they learned that they were in Colorado.

"Where you headin'?" the freighter asked later that morning as he surveyed their threadbare clothes and bruised feet.

"Denver," Zack said.

"Texas," Carrie said, correcting him. She looked at the man. "You ever heard of a man named Jefferson Davis Alder? Owns a big ranch in Prosperity, Texas?"

The freighter scratched his forehead. He was in his late twenties, short and powerful with a full chestnut-colored beard and nice hazel brown eyes. "Can't say as I have. Why you askin'?"

" 'Cause I'm gonna marry his son, Rio," she said, "if he is still alive."

The man, who had been sneaking sideways glances at Carrie, now looked at her in a peculiar way and drove on in silence.

When they came to the South Platte River, it was the widest, deepest thing that Zack could ever remember seeing. They came rolling down the north bank toward the river and the freighter said, "I have to pay a toll to the ferryman to take us across. I guess he'll charge you extra. Either of you got any money?"

"Nope," Zack said. "I reckon we'll have to get off and swim."

The freighter scowled and drove along for a few more minutes. When he reached the Platte, he glanced at Carrie again, saw the hollowness of her cheeks and the pinched suffering in her eyes. "Aw hell," he groused, "I reckon my company can stand your freight along with the rest of it. Neither of you looks thicker than a damn blade of marsh grass. I guess a big catfish might eat you both up, you're so skinny. I'll pay your toll."

"Thank you," Zack said warmly, for he had not been excited about swimming so swift and wide a river.

The freighter looked at Carrie, but she did not thank him. She did not even look his way and favor him with a smile. Her eyes reached beyond the Platte, farther even than Denver.

"She's sure got her mind on Texas," Zack said apologetically. "But I know she's as pleased as I am by your generous offer."

The freighter nodded but was not completely mollified. "I just hope she finds that Rio Alder feller," he grumbled, "for she won't be much company to anyone until she does."

They had no difficulty crossing the wide Platte and they continued on, angling along a well-traveled dirt track until nightfall when they made a dry camp on the prairie. The freighter, whose name was McWilliams, had plenty of water for the horses and even some firewood. He shared his food and coffee, but Carrie ate sparingly. As soon as it was dark, Carrie curled up beside the fire and fell asleep.

The freighter watched her so intently that Zack grew nervous. Even underweight and bedraggled, Carrie still possessed a haunting beauty and young women were scarce on the plains. The freighter's interest made Zack realize how much his sister's welfare depended on his ability to protect her against Godless men who cared nothing about the state of their souls.

Zack cleared his throat. The freighter looked strong, much stronger than himself. And the man had a gun strapped to his hip. Even so, it might be well to let him understand that Carrie was spoken for by Rio Alder.

"Mister," he said flatly, "if you are thinking about my sister the way I think you are thinkin', maybe we had better settle the issue right now. To get to her, you'll have to kill me and I will fight you tooth and claw."

The freighter blinked. Then smiled. "Young fella," he said, "you judge me unfairly. As a matter of fact, I was just thinking about my own wife and how her hair was also straw-colored, and when she slept, she sorta curled up catlike, too."

Zack felt ashamed. "I'm sorry, I guess I am three kinds of a fool."

"No, you aren't. That little sister is your responsibility. Do you really mean to take her all the way to Texas barefooted and without any money?"

"I do. And even if I did not, she would go on by herself. Nothing could stop her but dying."

"Nights are getting mighty cold on the trail, Zachariah. You aren't always going to have a friend offering you both a fire and food."

"We'll make out."

The freighter's voice took on an edge. "Don't be so damned stubborn," he said. "Do you even know in what part of Texas this Prosperity is to be found?"

"No."

"Jesus Christ!"

"Please be kind enough not to take the Lord's name

in vain,'' Zack said quietly. "It's breaking the second commandment, you know."

The freighter swore again, but to himself. "If you and her ain't just about the unlikeliest pair of babes I ever come across, I don't know who was!''

Zack was too weary to argue. "I guess I'll go to sleep now,'' he said. "And since you feel that way, I guess maybe we'll be gone when you wake up in the morning. Much obliged for all your help."

"Go on and get murdered then!" McWilliams yelled so loud it startled the dozing horses. He poked the camp-fire into wakefulness and poured himself some more coffee.

Zack could tell he was furious, but he did not under-stand why. Maybe it was just that the man did not know anything about self-determination.

"Mister, I need to ask you one more question before we go."

The freighter shot him an angry glance. "Go on then."

"What's your wife's name?"

McWilliams blinked and swallowed, and when he spoke, his voice had a strangled sound. "Her name was Pauline,'' he said. "She died of the pox two years ago."

"I'm sorry, I . . ."

"Go to sleep. But if you wake that girl and leave on foot, I'll whip these horses into a gallop and run you down like a couple of prairie chickens. Then I'll rope and tie you both and toss you into the wagon like sacks of potatoes. And you don't want to get your first glimpse of Denver over the tailgate of my wagon, do you?"

"No, sir,'' Zack said, "I don't believe so. Would you be good enough to answer just one more question?"

"If it ain't personal."

"It ain't."

"Then go ahead," the freighter sighed as if his patience had been taxed beyond normal limits.

"How far is it to Texas?"

"Jesus Christ," McWilliams breathed. "You really don't have any idea, do you?"

"Nope. But I sure wish you'd not take the Lord's name in vain."

"Texas is a long way."

"Two hundred miles?"

"More by far. But it all depends on just where Prosperity, Texas, is. If it's over near Houston, why, that's close to a thousand miles."

Zack gulped. He could not imagine such a distance. It would take him years to get Carrie that far.

"*But*," the freighter said, seeing the stricken look on his face in the firelight, "if Prosperity is up in the Texas Panhandle country, it might only be but three or four hundred miles."

Zack stretched out beside the fire. "I hope it is in the Panhandle then," he said with a yawn. "I am worried about getting our feet frostbitten if it snows."

The freighter stared at them for a long time. Then, finally, he rolled up in his soogans and stared up at the cold stars almost until morning.

Chapter Seven

"The thing about Denver," McWilliams was saying as they approached the bustling city, "is that it just refused to die. When I was a boy, my pa was a forty-niner. He and thousands like him heard of a big strike near Pikes Peak and half the prospectors in California came pouring across those Rockies. But there weren't much of a strike. Hell, it was mostly all talk. Land promoters is the only ones that got rich. But Denver was a natural place for a town, right there at the meeting of the South Platte and Cherry Creek. There was a promoter named Larimer and they named a street after him. He boosted Denver all over the country and the *Rocky Mountain News* said it was the finest and fastest-growing town on the central plains. People started believing that kind of talk, and even after the gold petered out, they stayed."

McWilliams pointed to a shiny pair of railroad tracks slicing northward. "See them tracks?"

"Yes."

"Well, a few years back everyone was saying that the new transcontinental railroad would make Denver the biggest town between St. Louis and San Francisco. But the railroad companies laid track a hundred miles to the north—up across Wyoming where you and Miss Carrie hail from. Denver should have died right then, but she didn't."

"How come?"

"Too much money already invested in the town," McWilliams said. "So the rich folks just decided to build their own damned railroads. They built that one clear up to Cheyenne and then they built the Denver and Rio Grande south to Pueblo! They about put freighters like me outa business. I reckon I ought to go to work for a damned old railroad, but I'm partial to wagons and horses. Steel and steam ain't got no heart."

"It sure is big," Carrie said softly.

McWilliams nodded. "You bet it is, little gal. And you'd do a lot worse than to settle here for a while. There's plenty of work. In fact, I know a few men who would probably give you both jobs."

Carrie shook her head. "That is not necessary, Mr. McWilliams. I've already told you that we are going to Texas."

"Well, how?" he asked with asperity. "You can't go traipsing across the prairie in your bare feet and without warm clothes. You got no food, nothing, not even a gun. What you need to do is find work and stay over this winter, save your money, and come spring, buy a ticket on the train down to Pueblo and then another on a stagecoach to Texas. Now, doesn't that make more sense?'' the man was almost pleading for Carrie to be reasonable.

It made plenty of sense to Zack, but he could tell by the set muscles along Carrie's jaw that—good sense or not—she wasn't waiting a minute longer than was necessary.

McWilliams snapped the lines and they popped dust clouds off the backs of his horses, sending them into a trot. "I swear," he grumbled, "I had heard that you needed to be half mule to be a sodbuster and I reckon you both qualify."

The freighter was still grumbling when he dropped them off on Larimer Street. "I know I shouldn't even concern myself with you and that little girl, but I'm going to offer one more piece of advice—no, three more."

Carrie stood waiting on the boardwalk. The street was jammed with freight wagons and men on horseback. Saloons lined the streets and Zack saw drunkenness and heard such cussing his ears grew red. He had never been in a place either as big or as busy as Denver; it was a little unnerving and he wished he and Carrie were back out on the quiet prairie.

"You aren't even listening to me!"

"Yes, sir," Zack said, watching two drunks brawl in the street while men passed them without even bothering to put a stop to the brutal spectacle.

"Then listen good, Zachariah Bennett, for your life and the life of that girl will depend on it. First off, you have to get some kind of outfit together or you will either freeze or starve to death. Second off, get a gun, any kind of gun, to protect yourself and your sister. Without being armed, you're sure to come to real grief. Can either of you shoot?''

117

"Both of us can."

"Good. And my last piece of advice is this, it's too late in the year to travel on foot. Stay in Denver until the spring and then hook on with a freighter heading down to Texas. Ask him where that damned Prosperity is located. That way, you'll be under his protection."

"Why would anyone want to give us protection?"

McWilliams shook his head with exasperation. "Hell if I know. But then, why am I working myself up into a hot lather worrying about you? There are other soft-headed men besides me and maybe you'll find another to help you." He stuck out his hand. "Good luck, Zachariah."

They shook. Zack wished he could have known the man better. "You ain't softheaded, Mr. McWilliams. You're just living the life of a Christian. Even if you are a cusser."

The freighter laughed outright. "Say a prayer for this poor sinner the next time you visit a church, sodbuster!"

And with that, he cracked his whip and moved into the city's flow with the other big freight wagons.

Zack and Carrie stood close together for a few minutes, and after McWilliams was gone, Zack said to his sister, "You wasn't too kindly toward him. He was just trying to help."

"Maybe. But he was also trying to tell us how to run our lives. People have been doing that for as long as I can remember. Pa, Miss Newby, the Reverend and even Ma. I'm tired of people telling me how to live, think and act. Mr. McWilliams was just another well-intentioned man trying to bend us to his liking, Zack. People like that will kill our self-determination every time."

"That might be true," Zack argued, not sure that she wasn't being much too hard on the freighter, "but he had some darned good advice just now."

"I couldn't hear for all the commotion around us. What did he say this time?"

Zack told her.

"He's finally right," she conceded, "we do need a gun and someone to lead us safely into Texas. But instead of a freighter, I say we tie up with a Texas trail driver, one that has just sold his cattle to those stockyards that we saw north of town. Then, we join him on his way back to Texas."

Zack thought that was a fine idea. He'd much rather go to Texas with a bunch of cowboys than some slow old freighters. Jostling along all day in a wagon was no fun.

"I wonder why Mr. McWilliams didn't suggest that," he said as they headed across town toward the stockyards.

Carrie smiled. "Because I'm smarter than he is," she said, "and because reaching Prosperity is all I can think about."

The Union Stockyard was huge, with acres of pens holding thousands of cattle. It took Zack almost an hour to locate the manager, a Mr. Elton Raison, and when he did, the man was so busy that Zack had to race along after his horse as he galloped around shouting frenzied orders to his stockyard hands.

On foot, Zack could see almost nothing, but it was clear things were not going well. Mr. Raison was mighty upset and yelling constantly.

"Hey," he bellowed, "you, Slim! Why can't you

boys read the damn shipping reports and get the right cattle into the right pens for the right railroads!''

'' 'Cause none of us can read,'' Slim explained in anger.

"Fer chrissakes," Raison yelled, "I got a bunch of illiterates working for me!"

Slim was burned. "Well, we can read brands and earnotches, by gawd! Why don't you put *them* on those worthless old papers!"

Raison cursed. He stopped to roll another cigarette and Zack caught up with him before he spurred on down another alleyway. "Sir," he pleaded, "aren't there any Texas drovers in town!"

The man glanced at him impatiently. "Why do you want one?"

Zack explained while Raison listened. He pointed to his sister and the stockyard manager nodded.

"Listen, farm boy," he said, "forget about Texas. You'll starve in Texas. Can you read?"

"Yeah, but . . ."

"Can that pretty sister of yours read?"

"Yes, sir, she's real smart but . . ."

"Then here!" He shoved the stack of shipping papers at Zack. "I'm giving you a job. See those numbers and those diagrams of the yard?"

"Sure, but . . ."

"Well, give your sister half them papers and read them and remember what they say because they explain everything right down to a gnat's ass. I got four thousand head of cattle that are supposed to be going north to Cheyenne tomorrow morning at daybreak. They are scattered all over this damned stockyard. I need some intelligent help, someone educated enough to read and follow orders.''

"But we're leaving for Texas!"

"No, you ain't. You're staying here and helping me. Tomorrow, I'll help you. Got it!"

Before Zack could answer, the man spurred away.

He walked back to Carrie, knowing she was not going to be pleased, but was agreeably surprised to find out that she was willing to help.

"One night's work for his help in getting us to Texas isn't so bad," she said, dividing up the shipping papers.

It was a long night, cattle and horses flying everywhere and cowboys cussing like crazy. Right away, Zack discovered that, being the only man on foot, he was fair game for both the cattle and the cowboys. It took some real fancy footwork to keep from getting trampled to death in the alleyways. But, somehow, they did the job, and when the train pulled out, the cattlecars were filled to bursting.

Zack and Carrie found Mr. Raison and the stockyard cowboys sharing a bottle of whiskey over a fine morning's sunrise. "Come have a drink, sodbusters."

"You said you'd help us." Carrie was all business.

"Yeah," Raison said, "I did for a fact." He studied them closely. "You two are hard workers, and smart. How'd you like to work here awhile?"

"No, sir." Carrie folded her arms across her chest. It was plain that she meant to leave within the hour.

"Think about it. I'll give you that shack yonder for your own, plus a dollar a day, plus all the beef you can eat. And I'll find you some good working duds and some boots, so you don't keep squeezin' cow plops up between your danged toes."

The cowboys thought the last part of his argument very humorous, but Carrie was not pleased. "The answer is still no."

"You're making a big mistake," Raison said with a shake of his head. "Miss, you are a pretty young lady, but you look winter-starved and in need of pasture."

"Well, this ain't no pasture and I ain't no heifer," Carrie said angrily.

Raison took another pull on the bottle and looked at Zack. "Talk sense into her. A mistake out on those plains is generally fatal."

Zack took his sister aside for a few moments of private conversation. "Listen," he said, "Mr. Raison has a fair point. We do need some new clothes and some shoes. And we need some money to buy a gun for protection."

When she still did not look convinced, he added desperately, "Rio is used to seeing pretty women. I didn't want to say this, but you look as if you had seen better days."

Her eyes widened. Involuntarily, she reached up and touched her hair. "Zack! When you're in love, you don't care about such things!"

"Well, maybe not. But you'll have to admit we're both pretty sorry-looking."

The seed of doubt was sowed and he watched it take root in her eyes.

Carrie paced back and forth with great agitation. "I wouldn't stay a minute longer than it takes to find a Texan willing to let us join up and go south."

"Of course not."

"And I don't want to work all night, every night, like we just did."

"I'm sure Mr. Raison was just in a bind and grateful to us for helping him out," Zack reasoned. "I think we ought to accept his offer."

"All right then, but only till the first Texans come riding in."

"It's a deal."

True to his word, Mr. Raison treated them fairly. The shack was fine and he paid them each a dollar a day and supplied them with enough fresh beef to feed five men and a lobo wolf. Zack figured they had never had things so good. There was no more night work once they had things running smoothly. The weeks passed quickly and Zack put on weight and marveled at how well Carrie looked again. They bought clothes, and on Sunday, they found a Methodist church and joined in with the singing and the congregating afterwards. At such times, Zack thought about his parents, and when he asked Carrie if she did too, she said no.

Fall was in the air before they realized it. All along the Platte and Cherry Creek, the trees turned brilliant colors and aspen shone like streaks of gold and ocher on the mountainsides. In the morning, ice thickened on the water troughs and they helped the cowboys break it with hammers so the cattle could drink.

But with fall came a restlessness that possessed Carrie so completely that she could hardly sleep at night. Zack could wake up anytime and discover her lying on her bed reading by candlelight or just staring up at the bare ceiling.

"What's wrong?" he finally dared to ask.

"There ain't no Texas trail herds coming through Denver," she said in a voice that trembled. "We've had 'em from the southern part of Colorado and from New

Mexico, even a couple from over in Arizona. But none from Texas.''

It was true. Zack hadn't thought about it much when they were busy, but now that the end of the trail-driving season was near, he realized that no Texas cattle had passed through Denver.

"I'm going to talk to Mr. Raison first thing in the morning," Carrie said. "I'm going to tell him that we are quitting and ask him what happened to the Texans."

Zack just nodded and went back to sleep. He had a strong hunch that, as things had gotten so slow these past couple of weeks, Mr. Raison was going to fire them anyway.

Carrie stood in the alley and glared at Mr. Raison, who was flanked protectively by his stockyard cowboys.

"You tricked us!" she cried.

"I did not."

"You did! Draw me Colorado, Texas and Chicago."

Mr. Raison shrugged and knelt. He smoothed the loose earth with his rough hand and then quickly poked three dots in the dirt. "This is us in Denver, that's the heart of Texas, and this here is Chicago."

"Where is Cheyenne and the Union Pacific Railroad?"

Raison drew that, too. "It runs all across the country."

"I know that." Carrie glared at him. "Now, show me where the Kansas Pacific Railroad runs."

Raison hesitated, then he drew a slash from Denver to Chicago and added three dots along its length. "Hays. Ellsworth. Abilene."

Zack stared in disbelief. Even a dummy could see that

nobody who planned to send cattle east would ever trail them west to Denver, when he could easily hook up in Kansas and save himself hundreds of miles.

"Damn that stupid Miss Newby!" Carrie shouted. "She made us memorize the capitals of every danged country in Europe and how to draw them, too! But she was so busy doing that that she forgot to teach us our own geography!"

Zack saw that it was the truth. Of course, they'd known that Texas was far south and a little to the east, but not *that* far. "Guess you really played us for a couple of fools," he said lamely.

Raison rolled a cigarette. "Sometimes education is a dangerous thing."

The cowboys roared with laughter, but it was not a mean kind. And maybe it was even overdue, since they'd been told they were ignorant and illiterate every day of the week.

"But I tell you what we have done," Raison said. "Me and the boys have pooled enough money together to buy you and Zack a couple of one-way tickets on the Kansas Pacific to Ellsworth. From there, you can hook up with a late trail herd coming up the old Chisholm Trail. Now, does that strike you as fair?"

"As fair as a summer day," Zack said, feeling deeply grateful. He looked at Carrie, who barely nodded. It was clear that she was miffed about being tricked into this delay, but it was also clear that it had been good for her. She had put on ten pounds and was almost her old, sassy self.

"Well, then," Raison said, "why don't we all have a little drink to say good-bye?"

This time, even Carrie took a sip.

*   *   *

The trip to Ellsworth, Kansas, was mostly uneventful. Zack had not known what to expect on a railroad, but what he discovered was that the day coaches were bumpy, smoky, drafty and overcrowded.

They sat in discomfort or tried to sleep on hard benches or on the floors. Being immediately behind the coal tender, they took the full brunt of the smoke from the engine and it made them sick to their stomachs. Their coach was crammed with passengers of every description. There were drummers and red-eyed gamblers playing cards in the aisles, women with crying babies, rough-looking men and two even rougher-looking painted ladies who had blue circles around the eyes and ruby-red lips and fingernails. Everybody with sense shunned them except for a particular drunken freighter who almost got his nose bit off for his forwardness.

Zack had never imagined such a collection of misfits and sinners all congregated together. The trip took a day and a night, and neither he nor Carrie closed their eyes a single minute. They had purchased two old revolvers, an 1851 cap-and-ball Navy Colt for Zack to wear openly, and at Carrie's insistence, a very evil-looking .44 caliber derringer. Zack had wanted to buy the newer model Colt Peacemaker that took cartridges, but Carrie had argued that they each needed a gun, and since the old black powder weapons were now considered antiquated, they could be bought cheap. Zack could not argue the fact nor could he deny that both cartridge and cap-and-ball weapons did the job if you hit what you aimed to hit.

Zack kept his gun loose in the cheap holster at his side, and he guessed that Carrie kept her derringer close at hand. Once, deep in the night as the train jounced along, he heard a scream at the far end of the coach and then he felt a long blast of cold air. In the morning, nothing was said, but the troublesome freighter was missing.

Kansas was as flat as a billiard table. Zack saw farms and sod houses by the hundreds—one was two stories tall. He saw cowboys and cattle, too, but it seemed to him that Kansas was going to the plow. And down in this lower latitude, he saw winter wheat that made his own Wyoming field look runty and brown cornstalks that stood higher than a man's head. Nestled in the bend of the Kansas River, he even saw a pig farm and that was a sight worth remembering. There must have been two hundred of the animals, and when the train huffed by and blew its long, mournful whistle, the pigs began to chase each other around and around in circles. It made him smile. Zack had asked his father to raise a few pigs, but Pa had always been afraid they would get away and the coyotes would eat them. Pigs, he'd said, were devilishly clever at escaping from pens, even more so than goats.

It was a happy sight when they pulled into Ellsworth, Kansas, though the town itself was nothing much to look at. It had especially wide streets and a stockyard that seemed to dominate the town. Cattle herds grazed for miles around Ellsworth, but here and there, he could see a few farms. Just before they disembarked, Zack heard a man saying that the farmers were fixing to quarantine the Texas cattle. The winter of 1871–72 had been awful and thousands of wintering longhorns had broken down farmers' fences, trampled their fields and eaten their precious winter hay. Anti-cattle forces were growing stronger each year in Ellsworth. The man looked out the window and said, "Give it ten, maybe even fifteen years, and you'll see the end of the long drive. Them damn farmers will have the whole range chopped up into so many little quarter sections of homestead land that even a thin coyote couldn't find a clear path up from Texas."

But his friend disagreed. "How they gonna fence it? No timber for fences, not even rocks like they use back East. No, sir, I tell you. Without fences, this land will be open right on through this century at least."

Zack agreed with the second man's assessment. As a farmer himself, he knew full well that, if a man could not protect his fields, he would lose them.

Carrie did not care. As the grumpy passengers grabbed their bags and stood, impatient to get off the smelly, uncomfortable train, her eyes were already searching the broad streets for Texas cowboys. And she saw plenty of them. Lean, sunburnt, swaggering young men who wore the same style hat, clothes and big-roweled spurs that Rio Alder and his men had worn.

Yes, she thought with growing excitement, here we *will* find men to take us to Prosperity. There will be no more waiting. No more delays.

When the conductor offered her his hand to assist her to the train platform, she ignored him and jumped down on her own, then started off at a brisk walk toward the stockyards with Zack in tow.

"Hey," he yelled, stretching his long legs out to catch her, "where's the fire!"

Carrie thumped her chest. "In here," she said, eyes riveted straight ahead. "I want to find the first crew that is leaving. I want to go south today!"

He grabbed her arm and slowed her up before they

hit the street. "Carrie, I have to ask you this. Has it occurred to you that Rio might not want to . . ."

She stopped dead in her tracks and turned on him. "Might not want to what!"

"Nothin'," he said, looking away.

Carrie hurried on. How could she explain the way it had been between herself and Rio? Words could not express how they had felt when they were together. The laughter, the holding hands, the wine and the clean tablecloths and . . . and sheets and pillowcases. Yes, all of it. There was no possibility of Zack understanding yet. He had never fallen in love. But he would some day and only then he would know when it was really real. She and Rio were made for each other. They even fit, physically and every other way. He had told her so and he was right.

Carrie knew that her brother feared that Rio had left her of his own free will, that he had used her for pleasure and then departed for home. That Zack would, for a single minute, consider that possibility hurt her deeply. But to try to convince him or Ma or Pa or anyone that something terrible had taken Rio away against his will was impossible. And yet she knew that Rio Alder loved her and would not have left her without being forced. The only real question was—had someone killed her Texas sweetheart?

There were times when she was sure that Rio was dead, so sure that she awoke in the night feeling as if her bones had turned to icicles and her heart to cold marble. At such times, she wanted to die, to just end it all and leave Zack free to find his own destiny. He thought he wanted to be a cowboy, but she was not so sure. He asked more questions about Kansas pigs and

Kansas corn than he did about longhorn cattle. And he always remarked on the color and richness of the soil and the grass, the way a farmer would. Perhaps it was that he just did not know enough about cattle to think of questions. Time would tell. Zack might remain a sod-buster forever.

But not her. The very smell of a newly plowed field turned her stomach. The sight of a plow or a sod house made her look away as if her eyes burned. It was funny. Zack had never shaken the sod from his heels, but she had scourged herself raw until she was finally cleansed, except for the memories.

To her, Ellsworth looked seedy. It didn't have the feeling of permanence she'd felt in either Denver or Cheyenne. It lacked character and charm. There were few trees, as if the people themselves did not expect to remain long enough to enjoy them. The buildings were poorly constructed, weathered, cracked and unpainted. The houses were not much better. This was a cattle town, and to Carrie's way of thinking, it bore a very strong resemblance to the infamous hell-on-wheels rail towns that she had read and heard about, the ones that had sprung like poisonous toadstools along the entire length of the transcontinental railroad. Carrie had a feeling that, like the toadstools, Ellsworth would soon wither and die.

"Hurry up, Zack," she said. "With those long legs of yours, you ought to be able to keep up easy. I got a feeling about this town."

"What kind of a feeling?"

"A feeling the sooner we leave it, the better."

Chapter Eight

The stockyard manager gestured toward a horseman sitting ramrod straight on a tall palomino stallion. He wore a black Stetson, a dark blue woolen shirt and split-cowhide vest, a pair of scarred leather chaps, and as his one fancy adornment, a set of beautiful silver spurs. They were large and embellished with intricate designs. The horseman was lean and weathered, though his thick brown hair told Carrie he could not have been much over thirty. Right now, he appeared totally absorbed in watching some cowboys separate a pen of rambunctious longhorn cattle.

"Miss, that there is Mr. Addison Wheeler. He's a big Texas rancher from down near Fort Worth. But he's not a man to traffic with sodbusters and farmers. Like most Texans, he heartily dislikes 'em for trying to block the cattle trails."

131

"We're not sodbusters anymore," Carrie said with an edge to her voice. "And my brother will soon learn to be a cowboy."

The man looked at Zack and it was clear from his expression that he was not impressed. "He's all farm boy now, though, and most cowboys have earned their spurs long before they was his age. Besides, Mr. Wheeler just sold his herd and ... "

Carrie turned her back on the man, who seemed much too eager to give her unwanted advice. As she approached the Texas cattleman, his dark eyes flicked toward her, and in a single glance, seemed to take her measure and then dismiss her in favor of the longhorns. It was not reassuring.

Because she intended that he become important to her and Zack, Carrie observed him closely. She noticed that Mr. Wheeler, alone among all the other mounted horsemen, had taken the time to shave and wear clean clothes. And even though they were frayed and worn, they were unmistakably well tailored and of excellent quality.

He shouted a man's name and ordered him to doctor a steer. There was an air of authority in his voice that reminded her of a military officer and Carrie immediately realized that his grammar was almost as correct as Miss Newby's. He had just the hint of a Southern drawl and she decided that he was probably well educated. Carrie remembered that, after the Civil War, many a young Confederate officer and enlisted man had left his beloved South to escape the hated Federalist reconstruction efforts and traveled to the wilds of untamed Texas. His palomino was almost as leggy as a Kentucky racehorse, though heavier in the shoulders and hindquarters.

Carrie had to crane her neck to look at him.

"Mr. Wheeler," she began, "my name is Carrie Bennett and this is my brother, Zack."

He looked down at her. "Forgive me, but I am occupied at the moment, Miss Bennett."

Carrie's cheeks colored. "I am sorry to interrupt your business, but my brother and I need to get to Prosperity, Texas. Do you know where it is to be found?"

"I do. It is just a day's ride west of Ft. Worth and not far from my own ranch." He might have said more, but suddenly, he wheeled his horse on its hind legs and spurred away, uncoiling his lariat at a dead run. Carrie saw a big longhorn steer break out of a pen and bolt for open country. The palomino overtook it before it had gone a hundred yards. Addison Wheeler's rope caught the horns and then he did something she had never seen before. The man flipped the rope around the steer's back legs and shot past the animal at an oblique angle. The steer's hind legs were cut out from under it and it crashed to the earth in a great cloud of dust.

"Did you see that!" Zack said with a low whistle of appreciation.

"Of course I did."

She watched as a Mexican vaquero wearing a huge sombrero and a colorful serape galloped out to Wheeler and the steer, shouted something in Spanish and then made a circling motion with his arm. It seemed he was both congratulating Addison Wheeler and at the same time demonstrating a refinement of the technique. Wheeler nodded, practiced the same motion once or twice and then answered the vaquero in the man's own language. The vaquero dismounted and slapped the dazed steer a few times across the muzzle until it revived. He then removed his employer's rope and replaced it with his own, which was enormously long and made of braided leather. The vaquero led the steer back to the stockyard as easily as if it were a puppy while the cattleman jogged his tall palomino back to survey the work. Carrie did not miss the obvious fact Wheeler was very deliberate not to rejoin them and continue their conversation.

"Do you think we should even bother to talk to the man?" Zack asked. "He doesn't seem very friendly."

"He can say no if he won't take us. But, according to the stockyard manager, he's the only one heading back to Texas very soon. And since he is going to within a single day's ride of Prosperity, I want to be with him."

Zack did not sound very hopeful. "I expect he'll refuse you."

"Maybe he will, at first," she said. "But something tells me that he was raised to be an officer and a Southern gentleman. I'll use that to our best advantage."

Zack would have liked to ask what the devil that was supposed to mean, but Carrie was already off again and so he followed. He had learned well enough that, when her mind was set, it was better just to go along and let events unfold.

"Mr. Wheeler," Carrie began a second time, "we *must* reach Prosperity."

"Why?" he asked. "That is cattle country, not farmland. There are enough settlers in Texas already."

Carrie had to swallow her temper. "We don't want to plow the land."

"That's right," Zack said. "I intend to be a cowboy."

Wheeler nodded with approval, but his inquiring eyes never left Carrie's face. "And what possible reason would motivate a young lady such as yourself to go to Prosperity?''

"To be with the man I intend to marry," she told him proudly. "His name is Rio Alder and his father's name is Jefferson Davis Alder. Are you acquainted with them?''

"*You* intend to marry Rio Alder?"

Something in the tone of his voice momentarily robbed her of speech. Was he going to tell her that Rio was dead? "Is something wrong?" she managed to ask.

"No," he said quickly, "I didn't mean to alarm you. It is just that the news surprised me. I know Rio and . . . well, I did not realize he had plans to marry.''

Rio *was* alive! Carrie felt almost weak with relief. "It all happened in Cheyenne," she explained. "And very suddenly. You see, he saved my life and we . . . we declared our love.''

"Then, congratulations." Addison Wheeler touched the brim of his Stetson and bowed his head slightly. "I wish you both great happiness.''

"Mr. Wheeler," she rushed, encouraged by his response, "we need someone to take us to Prosperity. And I thought . . .''

"I am very sorry," he apologized, cutting her off in anticipation of the request, "but I am afraid I must accompany these cattle to Chicago. I have already paid off my crew, except for Ignacio and a few other men who will drive some purebred stock and a few horses back to Texas for me. And they won't be ready to leave for several weeks.''

Carrie looked toward town. "I guess we can find someone else returning.''

"I'm afraid you might not," the cattleman said.

135

"Most of the cowboys you see will be holding herds here to winter or else they are working for big ranches in this area. Most of the Texans have gone home already."

Carrie felt crushed by this news.

"Miss Bennett, I would strongly advise you and your brother to remain here in Ellsworth, or even better, return to Cheyenne and wait for Rio to come for you. Write the man. It is much too dangerous a journey for two young people to undertake."

"We can take care of ourselves," Zack said defensively.

"I'm sure you can," Wheeler replied. "But there are still renegade Kiowa and Comanche to be dealt with along the Chisholm Trail and others who are . . . shall I say, in politeness to the lady . . . unsavory and ruthless."

Zack did not like the idea of a stranger telling them what they should or should not do. It was obvious that the Texan did not take him for anything but an inept sodbuster, one totally out of his element and too stupid to realize the fact. "I'd guess we'd hook on with someone returning to Texas."

"You might . . . and you might not," Wheeler said with a touch of exasperation creeping into his voice. "Can you justify risking your lives on such a possibility?"

"It's *my* decision," Carrie said abruptly.

The Texan nodded. "Yes, I can see that now. I'm sorry I can't help you. It is a long way to Prosperity."

"We have already come a long way," she told him. "Thank you for your precious time, Mr. Wheeler."

He touched his Stetson. "My pleasure, Miss Bennett. I just wish you would reconsider."

"I can't," she said in a small voice.

"I understand." He turned his horse and rode away.

"Come on," Carrie said tightly, "we have wasted enough time already."

"How much money have we got?" Zack asked.

Carrie pulled her thoughts together. "About twelve dollars."

"Then I think we ought to buy some food and leave immediately. We can walk ten miles before dark."

Carrie was surprised. She had expected Zack to want to remain here in Ellsworth until they found another trail driver. She wrapped her arms around her brother and hugged him, even though he squirmed with embarrassment. "I don't know if I'd have the nerve to walk to Texas alone."

"You'd do it if you had to," Zack answered. "We'll just be careful and watch for Indians."

Carrie agreed. She had thought that the Indian problem was a thing of the past. She had not even considered the possibility of unfriendly Indians between Ellsworth and Prosperity.

As they headed for the nearest general store, Carrie looked south in the direction of the Chisholm Trail that they would be following. It was just a huge swath of nearly grassless plain. Maybe it would be narrow and define itself as it funneled across Oklahoma and into Texas. Carrie did not think it possible that they could lose their way. But she decided that when they bought supplies, it might be smart to ask how far it was to Texas and if there were any big rivers to cross.

The Smoky Hill River just south of town was at its lowest this time of the year and they crossed it without any trouble at all. But as soon as they climbed up the far bank and gazed back toward Ellsworth, Carrie had such a empty and fearful feeling that she almost suggested they go back. She surmised that, if Zack had seen the desolation on her face, he would have guessed her thoughts and wanted to go back, too.

So she turned from him and shouldered her sack, concentrating on the simple fact of just putting one foot in front of the other. The rest of that day and then half of the next, they walked over earth grazed nearly clean and chewed up by thousands of cattle. They saw homesteads and cattle ranches and passed within just two miles of a big herd of longhorns. But then, suddenly, it was as if the earth had swallowed up all of humanity and before them lay nothing but short grass and long horizons. Carrie was accustomed to the vast empty spaces, but she had never experienced such a terrible sense of isolation as she did late that second day as they trudged along. It was made worse by the hollow sound of the prairie wind moving softly across the grass and the sky, driving huge, billowy clouds that stacked toward heaven.

"It's going to squawl," Zack announced, "and it's a good thing we bought rain slickers."

"I guess we had better use them to cover our sugar, flour and blankets instead of ourselves," Carrie said.

And so, when the sudden hard rain pelted from the sky, they knelt on the treeless plains holding their slickers down over their supplies so that they did not blow away. The raindrops were huge and cold. Carrie pulled her coat over her head and felt the lightning and thunderstorm shiver the earth. She prayed that they would not be struck and that the storm would soon pass.

Her prayers were answered. Within an hour, the racing storm front had swept eastward, driving the sky clear and polishing it blue and salmon. An apologetic sun, offering them fresh warmth, burned as it slid towards the curve of the earth. The grass steamed and rose again.

Just before sundown, they saw a line of trees far to the south and guessed it would mark the first big river they would have to cross, the Arkansas. Carrie remembered that the man at the general store had warned her that it was treacherous, especially after cloudbursts.

"I think we should walk to it tonight and search for a good crossing at daybreak," she said.

Zack just nodded. He had fallen into a silence like that of the land. Speech seemed unnecessary here. When he did not answer, Carrie turned her eyes south again and kept walking. She wished that she could duplicate Zack's smooth stride. His legs were considerably longer than her own and he seemed to cover the ground with half the effort.

Sunset was spectacular and they enjoyed it as they continued to walk. But the distance to the Arkansas River seemed fixed. The ragged line of trees did not grow until the moon had slipped into the sky and then, all at once, the trees were directly ahead and Carrie could smell the decay of the mud and marsh grass.

They tumbled wearily off the plains and slid down a steep embankment to face the dark, roiling water. Something splashed in the river and an owl floated silently past, then rounded a bend and was gone.

"It's bigger than I thought it would be," Carrie said, "a lot bigger. It puts Lodgepole Creek to shame."

"I guess it still ain't too big to swim," Zack said, not sounding very excited about the idea. "It's just going to be hard is all."

"Yeah," Carrie said. She spread out her blanket on the grass and collapsed on top of it in weariness. "Zack?"

"What?"

She watched him kneel beside the river and splash water on his face, then scrub the back of his neck. "You sorry you came with me?"

"No." He dried his face with his coat sleeve and came over to spread his blanket beside hers. "Why do you ask a dumb question like that?"

"I don't know. You've been sort of quiet for the last couple of days."

"I been thinking about how Mr. Wheeler roped that big longhorn and throwed him. And then how that Mexican came over and started telling him how he might have done it even better. I don't think I could ride or rope that good in a hundred years."

He spoke with such discouragement that Carrie realized how deep an impression the scene had made on him. "Nothing comes easy. When Rio and I are married, I expect he'll teach you how to rope like that. It'll just take practice."

"But you heard what that man said about how most cowboys are already good long before they reach my age. Maybe I'm too old to start."

"No, you're not," Carrie said. "That man talked too much and that's always the sign of a fool. Rio said you'd make a hand, didn't he?"

"Yeah."

"Well then, that's what'll happen."

She glanced over at her brother. His face was thoughtful as he gazed up at the stars and then he said in a forlorn voice, "Right now, it seems as if Prosperity,

Texas, is even farther away than those stars.''

Carrie reached out and touched him on the arm. ''I know. But it isn't. All we have to do is swim a few rivers and keep walking. You know how we used to live almost right on the old Oregon Trail. Why, there were little children and lots of women and old folks who walked that trail all the way across the country. Compared to them, what we have before us is nothing but a stroll.''

Zack shook his head and spoke to the distant stars. ''Carrie,'' he said, ''sometimes, you are damned near unbelievable.''

In the morning, they were dismayed to discover that the river had risen two feet and looked even more forbidding than it had in the moonlight.

''Maybe we should have swum it last night,'' Zack said.

''Uh-uh. Dark water scares me. If we have to, we'll wait until it goes down. Maybe we can catch some fish or shoot something to eat.''

Zack nodded, though he did not think it likely. They had, at the store owner's suggestion, bought line and hooks. He immediately set out to find worms, even though he knew that the river was too deep and swift to fish with bait. And as for shooting something, he saw nothing but small birds and muskrats. He did not think such poor game was worth the price of a bullet. He saw no deer tracks in the mud and the trees were untouched by the jaw of a beaver. Nevertheless, he decided to hunt downriver.

When he was gone, Carrie quickly stripped in the thick cover of willows and washed in the chill, muddy water. It was so cold she was covered with goose bumps.

The washing took her just a few minutes and then she redressed, feeling no cleaner. She knew that it was unlikely that Zack would either catch fish or find anything to shoot for meat, but she had decided that it would be better for his spirits to at least go through the motions rather than sit and contemplate the swift water and the loneliness of empty Kansas.

Carrie left her shoes with her blankets and started upriver. She guessed the Arkansas would recede, but she hated the idea of waiting. Maybe, she thought, it would be better if she followed the river a ways and searched for a wide spot where the current was not so swift.

The morning was cool and the trees along the riverbank blocked the warmth of the sun. She often came upon old campsites, some with busted whiskey bottles, empty tins and other trash left by white men, but there were others that she felt certain were used by Indians. At those camps, she found nothing but bone and ash. Staring at the Indian campgrounds, Carrie felt a shiver pass through her. She could close her eyes and almost visualize how the warriors might have crouched around the blackened ring of stones, roasting buffalo meat. And maybe they had captives, for who had not heard about the Comancheros and the terrible slave trade such men conducted south into Texas and even deeper, into Mexico.

The sun rose higher and she moved on, searching the river for a safe crossing. So intent was she on gauging the depth and current that she did not see the two riders watching her until they whipped their horses into the swift gray current.

The sound of the animals striking the river caught her attention. Carrie glanced up and her heart filled her throat. The men were like none she had seen in her life. They were big and dressed in mangy buffalo-robe coats that had patches of hair falling out. They carried rifles which they were using to beat their horses into the current. One man wore leather breeches and moccasins and the other had hightopped boots that reached to his knees. Both were bearded and so closely resembled each other that Carrie squeezed her eyes shut for a moment, certain that she was seeing double and maybe even gripped in a nightmare.

But when one of the horses floundered and tried to turn back, its rider slammed his rifle barrel across the crown of its head. The animal squealed and its head went under for a moment and then it rolled. The rider was thrown into the current. He hollered to his partner for help and that was when Carrie realized that they were very real and very intent on her capture. She did not wait to see if the swimming man was going to drown or be saved, she turned and ran for her life.

Branches and willows tore at her face and arms, and whenever she looked back, all she saw was empty river and that put even more fear into her heart. They had crossed! They were on *this* side and they were coming on horses!

She tried to shout for Zack to come and help her, but her breath was tearing in and out of her lungs and she knew that she could not stop to catch her breath. Too late, she realized how far she had wandered upriver. She tripped in marsh grass and spilled into the mud. Gasping, she scrambled to her feet and threw herself headlong through the willows and bushes, hearing laughter and shouts growing louder.

And then she saw their little camp and their blankets.

The sound of hooves cupping muddy ground sent her spinning around and she cried out, realizing that the hunters had almost overtaken her. She had left her derringer in her pack and that was what she wanted. But just before she could reach it, she felt the grassy breath of a horse as it swept in on her and then the air was being slammed from her lungs as she was kicked between the shoulder blades. She struck the wet grass and skidded into the muddy water. Stunned, she felt the current tug at her and she did not fight it.

"Grab her!" a man bellowed hoarsely.

Unable to get her footing in the mud, Carrie tried to roll into the Arkansas and take her chances, but the two men were flying off their horses and splashing into the shallow water.

She looked up and saw lust in their pitiless faces. Their buffalo coats were so rancid that she felt her stomach flop. They grabbed her and she beat helplessly at them. They laughed and she twisted free and threw herself into the swirling water, clawing to reach the swiftness of the current. Fingers locked into her hair and her face was shoved deep into the mud. She choked and swallowed water. A silent scream filled her chest as she was torn from the mud and the river.

All was lost. Her eyes and her mouth were filled with mud and she was dying, unable to breathe.

"She's chokin' to death, Zeb! Dunk her face again!"

Carrie felt them drop her back into the river, but she was too exhausted this time to try to escape. A hoary hand bruised her lips and scrubbed the dirt away, and when they yanked her head back, air exploded from her lungs and she was shocked to realize that she could breathe, but it was like inhaling flame. She heard their grunting laughter and felt their hands on her.

And then she heard the close, deadly blast of gunfire flat against the water. A scream and shots and more gunfire filled her ears. She heard a choking cough and felt water swirl all around her. Carrie opened her eyes. Smoke like fog rolled across the river.

''Carrie!''

It was Zack and he was dropping the old Navy Colt and running to her. She wanted to tell him not to let loose of the gun because of those terrible men. But she forgot her warning and closed her eyes, feeling the water closing in once more.

Zack stripped her to her chemise and then wrapped her in their dry blankets. Her dress was ripped from the neckline to the waist and he wanted to curse in anger as he tore a square out of it and then raced to the water to dampen and use it as a washrag. The two shaggy-looking bodies had finally been grasped by the swift Arkansas and they were no more than dark, bobbing specks on the river's surface. The horses, both very thin, were off a little ways, grazing.

Zack ran back up the bank and gently wiped gobs of mud from Carrie's face and hair. She was so white with cold that he could see the blue veins under her skin. If she caught pneumonia, she would die for certain. Not wanting to leave her in case she awoke and yet knowing he must, Zack dashed into the trees and quickly returned with bark and leaves. They were damp, but he still managed to get a smoky fire going and he nursed it into a healthy blaze. He ran back into the trees again and tore branches from them. He fed the fire until it grew hot and then he cradled his sister in his arms and rubbed her vigorously.

Carrie awoke with the taste of mud on her tongue. Her lips felt as big and ugly as caterpillars and her back as if it had been broken. But when she looked up at Zack, she took a deep breath and asked, "Are they dead?"

"Yeah, but I sure wished they could have died slower," he said in a shaky voice. "As God is my witness, I'm *glad* I killed them!"

"So am I."

Carrie sat up. "Go catch and hobble those horses," she told him, "before they eat their fill and run away."

"Will you be all right?"

She nodded. "You saved my life, Zack."

"You saved mine once, too," he told her. "Remember when I almost drowned?"

"Yeah." Carrie watched him go tend the horses. She did not even want to look at the river, for she was afraid she might see the dead men and start shaking, or worse. So she studied the flames and fed the fire until Zack returned with a canvas bag of jerky and a bottle of rye whiskey.

He uncorked the bottle with his teeth and took a long shuddering slug of the fiery liquid. It was only then that Carrie saw how badly unnerved he was and how he had begun to shiver now that the full impact of what had happened was hitting him.

"Drink some more," she said.

He considered the bottle carefully. "Pa always said this was the devil's brew. But that drink we had with Mr. Raison in Denver didn't totally ruin either of us."

"Pa is in Wyoming," Carrie said. "And the devil lost

two of his number just now. Have another drink. You earned all you want.''

Zack did drink and Carrie joined him. They drank too much and began to giggle crazily, half from the rye and half because something in them demanded they giggle and somehow balance the terror and the killing.

Zack fell asleep before the sun was straight up and Carrie arose to walk down to the river. She found the two rifles where the hunters had thrown them and they were good ones, too, both rimfire Henry repeaters—identical, like the men who had owned them. Carrie checked to make sure that they were loaded, even though she knew they would be. She went over to the horses and talked to them for several minutes until they stopped snorting and began to graze quietly once again. They were so skinny she thought they would eat for days if they had the chance. She checked their hobbles and then the saddles and outfits tied behind them.

Finally, she turned and really looked at the Arkansas River where she had almost drowned. Despite her urgent need to hurry on, she realized she could not face that water again today. Tomorrow. Yes, tomorrow would be better and she would feel strong again. And then, she and Zack would swim their new horses across the river and nothing would stop her from being reunited with Rio in Prosperity, Texas.

Chapter Nine

Zack awoke with the dawn, hearing something besides the rush of the Arkansas River. The sky was black except for a thin line of gray on the eastern horizon. The air was cold and damp. His teeth were chattering so loudly that they intruded upon his listening.

He cooked his head and then he realized that what had awakened him was the bawling of a cattle herd. Zack breathed warmth onto his numb hands, got up and buckled on his six-gun. Taking one of the Henry rifles, he left Carrie sleeping beside the river and hurried off to investigate.

He traveled a mile upriver before he realized that there were only about a hundred head of cattle and they were on the north side of the river, the same as he was. That puzzled him, for he had expected to find a herd traveling *up* the Chisholm Trail, not down it. By now the sunlight had grown strong enough that he could see more than outlines and silhouettes. These cattle were like none that he had ever seen before, white-faced and red-coated. Their horns were much shorter than those of Texas cattle and they were not nearly as tall, though certainly heavier. As he studied them, a rider emerged to gallop in his direction. Zack remained hidden. He saw a chuck wagon pulled by a team of horses, and when the lead rider was within a couple of hundred yards, Zack recognized both him and the tall palomino gelding that he rode.

"Mr. Wheeler!" he called, stepping out onto the flat plain and waving.

The man waved in greeting and loped to within a dozen feet of Zack. "I see you are waiting for the river to go down, Zack."

"We were yesterday, but not anymore. We have horses now, Mr. Wheeler. We plan to swim the river this morning."

Wheeler's eyebrows rose in question and he looked at the Henry rifle Zack was carrying but did not say anything. It took a few seconds for Zack to realize that the Texan was waiting for an explanation.

"Two men tried to get my sister yesterday. I shot them while they was in the river. We got another rifle just like this one and their horses and outfits."

Wheeler nodded. "Nice work."

Zack swelled with pride. "They didn't see me and they'd thrown down these rifles. I had them cold."

"That may be, but you didn't hesitate when the chips were down. You were right to shoot them without wasting words. Such men deserve no better. How is your sister feeling?"

"She's fit and still sleeping."

"No, I'm not," Carrie said, moving out of the trees with the second Henry resting across her forearm. "Your leaving woke me up, and I figured you might run into some trouble."

Zack felt a little miffed. "Well, I handled it yesterday pretty well."

Addison Wheeler dismounted and walked over to Carrie. "You look fine," he said.

"Thank you. What happened to your trip to Chicago?"

"I decided that could wait another year." Wheeler gestured back toward his men, horses and cattle. "These are called Herefords. They are an English breed of cattle that I intend to introduce into the longhorn blood."

Zack shook his head. "I never saw anything to compare to them. They all look exactly alike!"

"That's what Pokey said, at first. But after you've been around them a few days, you start to see the differences."

"How'd you come to try them?"

"My father first saw them at Henry Clay's farm in Kentucky when he brought them into this country way back in 1817. My father liked them so much he brought some down to our Virginia plantation. They're getting popular in the South and the North. I just hope they can stand up to the West."

"You better hope those fancy Thoroughbred horses can do the same," Carrie said, "but I wouldn't count on them making cow ponies."

Addison seemed surprised that she recognized the breed. Carrie decided not to tell him that, even though she might be the daughter of a Wyoming sodbuster, she had always had an eye for horses. There was a lot of horse racing being done in little towns around Cheyenne and the Thoroughbred was the preferred breed of betting men. Carrie found men amusing who thought that a farm girl knew nothing but how to cook, sew, shuck corn and raise children.

"I think my cowboys need some more size in their horses. There are a lot of people in Texas who will laugh at me and say that they are too fine-boned to stand up to the hard country down there, but this palomino of mine is half Thoroughbred and he's the finest all-around working horse I ever rode."

"We have horses," Carrie said.

"So I've been told. I'm sorry you had to go through so much unpleasantness to get them."

Carrie glanced away quickly. The thought of the two big men and what they had intended to do to her on the bank of the river was enough to make her weak in the knees.

"Miss Bennett, there will be others like them, maybe next time in greater numbers. It used to be the Indians I worried about in this country, but not anymore. There are Jayhawkers still running and more outlaws and misfits than you can count. I felt safer with the Indians. At least a man knew where he stood when he saw them."

"We now have good rifles," Zack said, his chin up and shoulders pulled back a little. "We can take care of ourselves."

"Oh, you've sure enough proven that," Wheeler said. "But if you still want to, I'd like you to join up with us. We are short a cook and a cook's helper. I could pay you each something and offer you the protection of our numbers."

Carrie turned to her brother. She saw stubborn defiance, and yet, she knew that it would be foolish to travel down to Texas alone.

"I want to accept the offer, Zack."

"I don't."

Addison Wheeler frowned as he looked at Zack. "May I ask why?"

"Because we can get to Prosperity, Texas, a lot faster without a herd of cattle."

"That may be true. However, if you run into renegade Indians, you might not get there at all. Besides, I thought you wanted to learn to become a cowboy."

"I do. That's the point. Lugging water and wood for Carrie sure won't improve my skills. I've already been doing that."

"I see. All right," Wheeler said. "When you aren't busy helping your sister, I promise that my men and I will help you learn a few tools of the cowboy's trade. Understand that learning to handle a rope from a man like Ignacio Valdez is not something to be sneezed at. The vaquero are the best ropers and horsemen you could ever hope to watch."

"Zack, please." Carrie knew that his pride was hurt. An hour ago, he had felt like a man who had been tested and had earned the role of her protector. Now, he was being asked to do a boy's job—for his own sister— which Carrie knew would be particularly galling. It was easy to understand his lack of enthusiasm.

He nodded. "Okay."

The Texan smiled. "Good! Then go get your outfits and join up with us. The river crossing is about eight miles downriver."

"Then what are you doing here?" Carrie asked.

Addison Wheeler muttered something as he swung into the saddle and then galloped away.

Zack frowned. "What excuse did he use?"

"I couldn't hear him either," Carrie said, considering. "Remember how I told you in Ellsworth I thought the man was raised an officer and a Southern gentleman?"

"Yes."

"His being here proves I was right."

Zack guessed that was true enough. He shielded his eyes from the bright morning sun and watched as the rancher rejoined his men, made a sweeping gesture with his arm and then pointed downriver.

"I guess we had best get our gear and go do whatever it is we are supposed to do," Zack said a little morosely. "Probably the best thing I can do is to stay right far out of their way until quitting time."

Carrie smiled with understanding. "You'll do fine. Just remember this—not a man among them can build a sod house or plow a straight furrow or handle a team of oxen."

"Now why should any of them want to know darned fool things like that?"

"How should I know? But remember how those cowboys at the Union Stockyard in Denver looked up to us?"

"That was because we could read and write and they couldn't. What's that got to do with anything out here?"

"Beats me. But the fact is we came all the way from Wyoming with nothing but the clothes on our backs. We walked and we rode trains over five hundred miles. We earned our keep and then you killed two men who needed killing. It seems to me we have nothing to apologize to anyone for. It seems to me we'd have made it to Prosperity with or without Mr. Addison Wheeler and his cowboys."

"Then why didn't we try?"

"Because," Carrie said, "only a fool takes foolish chances when he can do things safe. And we are not fools. You'd have seen the sense of his offer and accepted it before that herd crossed the river. And then you'd have been man enough to swallow your pride and tell Mr. Wheeler you'd changed your mind."

"I ain't so sure," he said, falling in with her as they headed for their camp.

"The thing about you, Zack, is that you always underestimate your abilities. I used to do the same thing—until I fell in love with Rio. He taught me how special I was. That was something that Pa never did with Ma. He just spouted the Bible and made us all feel like sinners. You know what would have happened to me if I'd stayed at the homestead, or even in Wyoming."

Zack nodded. He'd thought about it plenty.

"Pa . . ." Carrie took a deep breath. ". . . Pa branded me a whore. I could have lived the rest of my life more pious than a saint and it would not have mattered. I would have always been a whore to him and to the rest of our church congregation."

"Not to Ma and me, you wouldn't."

Carrie took his big hand. "No," she said, "you understood. And you knew that I would have withered and died like a rose in the winter had I stayed. I can't go back."

"I know."

Her expression grew hard and her voice shook with bitterness. "I could *never, ever* go back home! I'd sooner be dead. I would be a living dead person if I went back home.''

Zack squeezed her hand and glanced sideways at her. He did not like to hear her say such things and the expression on her face bothered him plenty. Yet, he should not have been surprised. Pa had always been too hard on her and Ma had never had enough gumption to interfere.

''You'll never have to go back,'' he promised. ''Let's get this camp broke and go meet the crew.''

If the two cowboys and two vaqueros thought it strange to see a sodbuster in bib overalls, heavy work boots and a bright yellow cowboy's bandanna riding beside a pretty young woman with purplish, swollen lips and wearing a man's clothes, they did not say a word or so much as raise an eyebrow.

Addison Wheeler introduced them to Pokey Joe Salisbury and Snorty Watson who were both in their fifties. Pokey Joe was the chuck wagon driver and probably had been the cook up until now. The man talked so slowly, it was plain to see how he had received his nickname. He was heavy-lidded and wore a perpetual smile. Snorty was almost his opposite. Short and intense, he wore his gray hair in a small ponytail at the back of his neck under the brim of his hat and nervously chewed and spat a continuous stream of tobacco.

Ignacio Valdez and Ramon Escobar were both much younger, shy and soft-spoken vaqueros who understood English but spoke just a few salutations, and Zack was soon to discover, a nice string of cuss words. Their sombreros were so large as to be almost comical, but they had beautiful hatbands bedecked with silver coins. They wore brightly colored serapes and their pants were also ornate, with fancy embroidery work on the fabric. Their spurs had such huge rowels that when they walked they clicked and dragged the ground, leaving twin trails of dots in the dirt. Even their saddles were extravagant, with enormous horns and stirrups covered with flared leather tapederos. Altogether, the American cowboys and even Mr. Wheeler looked downright drab in comparison.

"Compadres," Wheeler said, using the Spanish word to address all four of his men, "this is Señorita Carrie Bennett and Señor Zack Bennett. They will be helping us out."

Zack noted the grave formality of the men who nodded to him and Carrie. Despite his own shabby dress and the sad condition of their horses, he saw nothing to indicate that they were held in low esteem. In fact, it almost seemed a little bit the opposite. Zack could only guess that Wheeler had told them about their journey from Cheyenne and even about the two hunters he had killed in the Arkansas River.

"I guess we might as well get to the crossing and swim that big river," Wheeler said. "Zack," he added quietly, "do you suppose you can handle a team any better than Pokey Joe? I'm half afraid to have him drive our chuck wagon down into all that fast water. That wagon has all our food, supplies and bedrolls. We'd be in a bad fix if it spilled into the Arkansas."

Zack nodded and tied his horse to one side of the tailgate while Carrie tied hers to the other. "I can handle a team," he said, just now realizing how important a role he had been assigned, "and so can Carrie. We'll get it across in good shape."

Pokey Joe looked genuinely grateful as Zack and Carrie took his place on the wagon. A moment later, he had his saddle out of the wagonbed and on the back of a roan. Once mounted, he somehow looked much younger, and when he galloped away, Zack guessed him to be no more than thirty years old.

They crossed the Arkansas River without any trouble, though the Texan commented that the purebred Herefords did not swim nearly as well as Texas longhorns.

Riding along beside the wagon late that afternoon, Wheeler said, "As far as cattle go, the longhorns are the best animals nature could have created for the frontier. They can swim like seals, run like deer and fight like a den of mountain lions. They can travel all day and cover more miles on less feed and water than most horses."

"If they are all of that," Zack asked, snapping the lines to keep the team stepping along, "then why introduce the Hereford blood?"

"Because the only failing of the longhorn is that its meat is in short supply and as tough as its hide. The longhorn may be king of the western range but it's dead last when it comes to eating. Even as a boy, I recognized the difference between the steaks the European breeds produce and those that the longhorn will give you. And as more and more Texas cattle come up the trail in the years ahead, the people back east will finally start getting enough beef to become choosy. Mark my words, they'll sure pay a premium to a cattleman who has introduced a little European breeding into his herds."

"Were you an officer in the War?" Carrie suddenly asked.

"Why, yes, a captain with the Army of Northern Virginia. How did you guess?"

Carrie shrugged her shoulders. "Just a thought."

He looked at her, his brown eyes frank and appraising. Then, tipping his hat, he galloped off to scout ahead.

"He sure didn't change his mind about going to Chicago for my sake," Zack said with a slow smile. "I think he's taken with you, Carrie."

"Oh, bosh! That man knows I'm betrothed to Rio Alder."

"You ain't wearing no engagement ring."

"That doesn't matter at all!"

Zack clammed his mouth shut. He had said the wrong thing, but he could tell that Addison Wheeler was thinking his sister was pretty and maybe sort of special.

Heck, Zack thought philosophically, if Rio Alder won't marry her, maybe Addison Wheeler will.

They had forded the Cimarron and were almost in sight of the Canadian River. Zack was riding one of the Wheeler Ranch horses, a spunky sorrel mare that bucked him off every morning, but with increasing difficulty.

Addison had given him an extra grass rope from the supply box and Zack was following Ignacio's roping instructions to the letter. The first throw that Ignacio taught him was called a *mangana* and it was an underhanded toss that the cowboys used to snare a cow pony who refused to be caught early in the morning. The mangana delivered a loop that snaked out like a fist and caught the horse by the forefeet. The roper then took a half-wrap around his hips so that, when the horse struck the end of the rope, it suddenly found itself crashing to earth. Because of the danger of injuring a good horse's neck or shoulders, Mr. Wheeler did not allow that loop to be used on the Thoroughbreds. Rather, they were caught with an overhand toss managed without twirling the noose even once. One minute, the man would be standing near a horse, the next the rope would sail out and drop over its head.

The two cowboys were expert with that toss, but they were not nearly as adept with the mangana as were the vaqueros. There were other loops that a good cowboy had to learn, in addition to simply tossing out a huge Blocker loop and hoping to catch a set of horns. Zack was most in awe of the *peal* loop, a word that means "sock" in Spanish. It was so named because, when thrown, the rope would form a figure eight, each loop capturing a rear foot. Zack practiced it for hours on end as they rode along, but the figure eight would never come out right. So mostly, he just practiced heading on bushes and heeling on the Hereford cows who soon became indifferent to his pitiful attempts.

Addison also taught him little things about cattle, how to watch them for signs of trouble, of sickness or contrariness. He maintained that a good cowboy would quickly learn the faces and personalities of every member of a big herd of cattle. And if one was absent in the morning, it would be missed immediately.

The days passed quickly and pleasantly. It became apparent that Addison had not needed their help at all and the five Texans had been plenty able to handle the small herd and band of horses. Zack soon decided that cowboying was about the easiest thing imaginable. After he helped Carrie with the breakfast and repacking the wagon, he was free to ride with the cowboys up until evening. In an attempt to be more like them, he cut off the top of his bib overalls and fashioned a belt of sorts, fancying that he didn't look so much like a sodbuster anymore.

While crossing the eastern edge of the Red Hills country, Ignacio had found a genuine Stetson hat up in the topmost branches of a big thicket. It was a danged nice one, too, black felt with the seller's name, E. J. HOLLOWAY, AUSTIN, TX., stitched in the inside band alongside the word CARLSBAD, which was the style preferred by Texas cowboys. It was pretty banged up and dirty, but that didn't bother Zack half as much as the fact that the inside band was smeared with black, crusted blood.

Ignacio and Ramon spent a couple hours searching for the owner of the hat or his remains but came up empty. Pokey Joe and Snorty Watson already had good Stetsons, so it was Zack's for the taking and everybody agreed that the hat must have cost its owner nearly a month's wages. Yet, for two fretful days, Zack refused even to try on the hat because of the blood, but when Carrie cleaned the band and chided him for his foolish superstitions, he relented and was pleased to discover that the hat was a little too small. It was just the excuse he needed to justify cutting out the offending inner band so that his new Stetson fit perfectly. And as for the blood and the possibility that the hat might be jinxed, he went along with Pokey Joe, who reckoned that it would be a mighty unusual hat that would see two of its owners come to grievous ends.

By the time they swam the Canadian, there was frost on the ground every morning, and in the daytime, the temperatures were often no more than sixty degrees. Addison had skirted a little to the east in the hope of missing Indian Territory altogether, but his hope was dashed when, only an hour before sundown and with biscuits and beef filling their tin plates, they were approached by a large number of Comanches.

Zack was so startled that he dropped his food in the dirt and reached for his gun, but Snorty Watson was close enough to grab his wrist and shove the old Navy Colt back into its holster.

"Steady up, young feller!" Snorty snapped impatiently. "Let Mr. Wheeler handle them."

Zack eased over beside Carrie, who was as unnerved by the scene as he was. The Comanche were bigger men than he had expected and they rode fine horses. There were at least a dozen and they all had rifles, though some looked to be ancient muzzle loaders of a kind that Zack had not seen since he was a small boy.

Snorty read his thoughts and whispered, "Them Indians can use those old percussion rifles better'n you'd think. I seen 'em fire and reload the damn things at a full gallop, shooting over the back and under the neck of a horse. They hold two or more balls at a time in their mouths and spit the danged things down the muzzle after sloshin' in a charge of fresh powder from their horns. Don't you be taking them lightly, Zack."

"No chance of that," he said.

"What's Mr. Wheeler going to do?" Carrie asked as she watched Addison making sign language with the Indians.

Snorty glanced at her with an expression of pity. "I'm afraid he's inviting them for dinner, Miss Carrie."

"Dinner!" she cried. "Are you serious!"

The sign language stopped and the Indians all stared at her. Carrie felt like crawling under the wagon. She forced herself to say loudly, "Oh, dinner for our guests, how nice!"

Addison grinned. "Glad you feel that way. Make some more biscuits. Lots of them. And plenty of strong, hot coffee. They'll be offended if they can't have coffee with their roasts."

"Roasts?" She was appalled.

"Ignacio!"

"*Sí!*"

"You and Ramon kill and butcher that old cow and her heifer. You know which ones."

"*Sí,*" he said, as he turned and grabbed his rifle and a knife from the cutting rack.

"Zack?"

"Sir?"

"Get a big fire going right over there." He pointed off to the west about a hundred feet. It would put their camp between the reservation Comanche and the Thoroughbred horses which the Indians were viewing with great interest.

"Miss Bennett," he said, "you might be better off to rest in the wagon this evening. These are not raiders, but they can be trouble if excited."

"I would not excite them," she said. "That is the very last thing that I would do."

"Suit yourself. Pokey, you and Snorty move the Thoroughbred horses and the Herefords off a little behind that hill and stay with them until I call."

"That'll just leave the five of you to watch this whole bunch of thieves."

"We will do fine."

"Yes, sir."

Carrie supposed that she should have been glad to get

into the wagon, but it was obvious that her eyes and ears were needed to watch the Indians and avoid wholesale pilferage.

Two quick rifle shots sent heads turning around and the Indians headed toward Ignacio, Ramon and the dying Herefords in a mass exodus.

Carrie stepped up on the iron rim of the wagon wheel so that she could see better. She watched Ignacio and Ramon fall upon the quivering Hereford cow and calf with their knives. The Comanche crowded in close to watch and offer excited instructions in their language. One of the leaders could not restrain himself. He drew his knife, knelt beside the cow and split her belly wide open. Then, to Carrie's horror, the Indian reached inside of her and yanked out the entrails and began hacking them into slippery segments. He stuffed the first one into his mouth, then retreated as others crowded in and began to gobble up the raw intestines.

Carrie twisted away. Later, with her stomach still queasy, she helped Zack build a new camp fire for the Indians. They were low on wood and she began to collect cowchips. There was no shortage of those. As far as the eye could see, the prairie was covered with grass and cowchips. Once, she supposed, it would have been buffalo chips, but they were gone and all that remained of the buffalo were occasional old bones and skulls, a horn, and the huge buffalo wallows that had cratered the land all the way south from Ellsworth.

The Indians were covered with gore and satiated with entrails even before the beef and biscuits were ready. Still, Addison cut huge steaks and roasts. He seared them on the outside, leaving the blood and juices inside, explaining as he worked, ''They'll eat again around midnight and take what is left in the morning."

"You mean they are staying the night!" Carrie was shocked.

"That's right. But over in their own camp, not here in ours. I made that much plain."

"Thank heaven!"

He touched her on the shoulder. "It was good of you to help instead of hide in the wagon. I should have warned you about their dining habits, but I forgot. Besides, they are usually a little less exuberant. In the summer when the herds are passing nearly every day, they will just take a few head and trail them to their village before the slaughter. But at this time of year . . ."

"They are starved-looking," Carrie said. In fact, she had noticed their shocking thinness right away.

"Yes." Addison shook his head. "They don't get the food they should on the reservations. The Plains Indians have never condescended to farm. And without corn to store for the winter, they are pretty much reliant on the Indian agents. And *that*," he said with an edge to his voice. "is a poor position to be in."

"I see." Carrie checked her biscuits. When they were ready, she steeled her nerves and served them. She had made at least two dozen, but they vanished down the throats of the Comanche before she finished moving among them. She returned to her Dutch oven and made another batch, and later two more.

The Indians did feast again; they ate as if they had not had food in weeks. Carrie and Zack went among them and poured coffee though she only had nine cups. It was long past midnight before the Indians began to curl up on their blankets and fall asleep right where they had eaten.

"I've never seen the likes of it," she said as she stood beside Addison and their own campfire. "I expected to be frightened to death by them and . . . I feel more pity than anything else."

The cattleman nodded. "It is sad. At times, I have seen them so hungry that they have begged for scraps. When I first came to Texas, they were a proud, free people who followed the buffalo herds and asked nothing but to hunt and trade and make war on their enemies as they had for centuries."

"You admire them." Carrie said it without question. It was obvious that he did.

"Yes. And respect them for their cunning and fighting ability."

That night, Carrie slept uneasily. She dreamed of Indians and entrails and awoke several times feeling as if she was going to choke. When dawn came, she could smell meat cooking. And shortly after that, the Comanche were gone.

Chapter Ten

They were almost to Texas. Zack awoke and pulled on his boots, shivering in the thin, predawn light. The moon was still low in the eastern sky, just a yellow crescent suspended against a blue wall.

Zack got the fire going and listened to thunder rumble across the Oklahoma sky. It was cold enough to see his breath and he was damned glad that this long ride was nearly over. The ground seemed frozen and his bones were so stiff every morning that he felt sure they would crack if he used them too suddenly.

He heard Carrie cough and then crawl out of bed. She had held up well on the Chisholm Trail, until the weather had turned frightfully cold during the past two weeks. Now, she had a wracking cough. Both he and Mr. Wheeler had practically begged her to stay in bed and let him do the breakfast cooking. But she wouldn't.

She was just too pigheaded to listen to anyone.

Zack filled the coffee pot and set it on a grate to boil. He cut slices of beef and had them frying by the time Carrie was able to join him.

"Look at that sky," she said, as the gray light struggled up from the east. "I'm afraid we are in for a storm, and a bad one, from the looks of those thunderheads."

Addison Wheeler rode in from the herd. He stood night watch just as if he were a hired hand and many times Zack had gotten up in the dark and ridden out to keep him company. They had, during those long, starlit hours, become close friends.

He stepped down from his horse and touched the pot of coffee. Finding it still cold, he turned and said, "Zack, I'm worried about the storm. The Red River is just five miles ahead and if we get caught on this side of it before a big rain, we could be stranded here a week or longer. That's why I need you to help us push the cattle and horses hard this morning. We are going to cross the Red, come hell or high water."

The other men were already up and pulling on their boots, jackets, chaps and gloves. One look at the threatening sky told them better than words that they had to cross the Red in a big hurry.

"Coffee will be ready in just a few minutes!" Carrie shouted.

"Can't wait." Wheeler remounted. "Zack, help her break camp. We can have our breakfast in Texas later on, if all goes well. There is no more time to waste."

Zack grabbed the pot, pitched coffee and cold water onto the fire and tossed the pot into the wagon. Bedrolls came flying in, too, and then, while Carrie hurried

167

around gathering up last night's cooking gear, Zack tried to rope the horses.

The remuda was frightfully skittish. Zack tried to catch the team, but every time a bolt of lightning struck the land, they went half crazy. Pokey Joe and Snorty weren't having much luck either and they did not complain when Ignacio and Ramon used their long leather reatas to catch all the horses. Hard drops of rain were beginning to strike. The wind picked up so that the drops felt like ice and came in so flat that their Stetsons protected nothing below their eyebrows.

The cowboys and vaqueros left on the run. When Zack finally managed to get the team hitched to the chuck wagon, he handed the lines to Carrie. The team was fighting to outrun the storm and Zack shouted into the wind, "Let 'em run in the face of it, Carrie. That's what we'll be doing with the herd!"

Ignacio had hobbled Zack's sorrel mare, saving him the embarrassment and wasted time of trying to catch her. Zack saddled quickly, his fingers numb, his mind racing. He had to struggle to get his boot into the stirrup because the mare was spinning around in great excitement. Carrie and the chuck wagon shot off into the storm.

"Dang it!" Zack yelled, desperately throwing his leg up and almost losing his balance before he grabbed the saddle horn. "Settle down!"

But the moment his right boot was thrust into the stirrup, the mare exploded into a bucking fit the likes of which he had never seen nor felt. Zack wore spurs now and he was so angry he used them on the fool mare. Buffeted by wind and rain, the man and the horse fought each other like blind things. The mare used every trick it had and—for once—her tricks failed. Not only did the man stick, but he punished her with his spurs and soon the mare dipped her pretty head and gave up the fight. Steam was boiling off her wet coat and Zack roweled her into a flat-out run.

He swept past Carrie and soon overtook the herd. The remuda of Thoroughbreds had never before shown any interest in scattering or leaving the camp. But now the blooded horses were a mile ahead of the cattle and rapidly vanishing toward the Red River. Zack could just see Wheeler, Ignacio and Ramon riding hard in their wake.

Pokey Joe was waving frantically for him to help Snorty Watson keep the herd racing for the river. Zack felt the earth shake as a huge bolt of lightning crashed into a grove of trees off to the west and lit up a big patch of sky.

Hail began to pelt them. It came down hard and fast, bigger and bigger, until it was the size of chicken, then duck, eggs. Zack cinched his Stetson down even tighter, but every hailstone felt as if it were a piece of hurled granite. He raised his forearm over his eyes, knowing he could be blinded for life.

The sorrel squealed in pain as stones bounced off her sleek coat. She fought the bit and threw her head wildly. But there was nothing he could do except stick in the saddle while the storm raged with growing intensity.

The Herefords alone seemed oblivious to the hail. They ran on as if pulled by invisible strings toward the Red River. Once, Zack twisted around in the saddle to see if Carrie and the chuck wagon were still coming. But the hail beat against his face so severely that he gave up.

On and on they raced; the prairie became a slithering white table of ice and then, suddenly, there was a line of trees and the land was dropping toward the river. The Herefords could not, would not, stop. They threw themselves across the low muddy banks and then hit the river like a tornado. Zack felt his sorrel stumble. He yanked hard on the reins, and somehow, the animal stayed on its feet. Too late, the mare realized she was going into the Red. When they struck the water, Zack was surprised to discover that it was one hell of a lot warmer than the air.

Mr. Wheeler was across but coming back. Pokey Joe had his rope out and was furiously whipping a lead bull that had decided, at midstream, to return to Oklahoma Territory. Zack saw the herd try to turn with the leader. There was a chance they could go into a bad mill. Ramon and Ignacio were fighting to keep them straight. Snorty Watson's horse was struck by a huge branch and bowled over.

Mr. Wheeler went right after him. Zack saw the rancher shoot his rope out to Snorty, who grabbed it and dallied around his saddle horn. The momentary jerk of the rope seemed to right Snorty's floundering horse and it finally broke free of the big branch, but, by then, Snorty and the boss were far downriver and unable to help.

Zack spurred the mare hard and felt it swimming for its life. They were sandwiched into the cattle now and he realized his mistake. He was helpless to do anything but hang on and pray to God that the herd soon struck the Texas shore.

It did. When the sorrel's hoof hit the mud, Zack felt its body hump and then claw for footing. A few seconds later, they were scrambling out of the water and the herd was flowing up the bank to scatter. Zack followed Pokey Joe and the vaqueros. He was so cold and scared he could not even let go of his saddle horn.

Still a mile north of Red River, Carrie discovered that ice and mud had rendered her brakes absolutely useless. She kept yanking on the lines with her left hand and sawing on the brake with her right, but nothing was happening. Behind her, she could hear cooking utensils clanging and banging. She also heard her water barrel crash to the earth and disintegrate. The latch on the tailgate table had given way; when she glanced over her shoulder, it was down. That meant that all of her pots, pans, plates, and Dutch ovens were gone, along with the coffee pot and eating utensils.

Dammit! Even her hat was gone and the damn hailstones were beating her face raw. She could taste blood on her lips, and though she tried to keep her head bent downward, nothing seemed to help.

If she had any sense at all, she would just throw the lines up in the air and fall back under the protection of the canvas. But that would rob her of any chance of saving the wagon.

So she stuck to her seat and suffered the flying mud and hail until she was nearly blind, took it until she felt the wagon suddenly lurch downward and then go careening over the river bank. A scream filled her throat as she felt herself being lifted high into the air and then slammed into the Red. Memories of the Arkansas River and the two dead hunters who had held her face underwater swirled up to fill her with mindless terror.

The Red was swift, swifter even than the Arkansas. She was driven under its powerful current and instinctively thrashed and churned upward toward the pelting hail. Her head cleared water and she was immediately pulled under again. But once more she clawed upward to face the dim light of day and then Addison was driving his horse in close and his strong hands were pulling her across the animal's neck. Carrie clung to the animal and finally rejoiced in the feel of solid ground against her back. Addison bent over to shield her from the hailstones.

"I lost the chuck wagon," she whispered, her teeth rattling like dice. "I lost everything!"

"It doesn't matter!" he shouted, his breath warm on her face. "I don't give a goddamn about the wagon. You're all that counts!"

He pressed down on her in the mud. She clung to him and listened to the storm until it passed.

Carrie wished that Addison Wheeler had not spoiled everything by saying what he had said. When the storm was over and the livestock finally gathered, she sat forlornly beside the Red River and tended a small, smoky camp fire. Addison had taken Snorty Watson back across the river to retrieve as much of their scattered food and supplies as could be found. Carrie had asked for the Dutch oven, a frying pan and the huge old coffee pot she had tended so faithfully these past weeks. She hoped maybe a side of beef or something edible could be found, but doubted if any of the flour or sugar would be salvaged. The hail and the rain would have ruined it.

She kept glancing down at the rain-swollen river as if the swift red water might suddenly regurgitate the chuck wagon about which she had grown so possessive. But the wagon was gone, the four team horses drowned in their harness. Zack had reported that what was left of the wagon was scattered down both sides of the Red for miles. The horses were all tangled up in a tree right out in the middle of the river, just as she would have been, had it not been for Addison.

But dammit, he loved her! And she loved Rio Alder. That made her very sad. Carrie could not imagine loving someone as much as she did Rio and then discovering the person did not love her back. She wished that Addison had not told her. It made everything so much more difficult and now, whenever he looked at her, she knew she would feel rotten.

How could he have let something like that happen! Hadn't she told him plain out that she was going to Prosperity to marry Rio? And the fool had fallen in love with her anyway. He ought to have known better than to do something that stupid. But then, she had fallen for Rio the moment he had saved her life that day in the streets of Cheyenne and he had not loved her until . . . well . . . until they had known each other as man and woman. So, she guessed that if Rio had not conveniently fallen in love with her, she would be in exactly the same sorry state as Addison.

Apparently, love could get very complicated. Only now did Carrie realize that it was a fortunate thing indeed when two people loved each other equally.

Zack rode in from the herd. "You look awful," he said, dismounting to stand in the mud.

She glanced up at him. "You don't look so good either."

He frowned. "Mr. Wheeler said you did a hell of a job just to reach the river. Said not many people would have even stayed with that chuck wagon like you did."

"I'd have jumped, for Chrissakes, if it hadn't been going so fast!"

"But you didn't."

Carrie looked up at him again and started to say something but she began coughing so hard that she forgot what it was. When she coughed, it felt as if a bunch of red-hot needles were jabbing the insides of her lungs. She had trouble getting her breath. She coughed up big gobs of phlegm and that worried her because she knew the damned awful stuff could fill up her lungs like water and she could suffocate.

Zack waited until her fit of coughing finally died. "Mr. Wheeler says we don't need the chuck wagon anyway. His ranch is only eighty miles south of here and he sent Ramon for a buckboard that you can lie in."

"I don't want to ride on my back in a buckboard!" she cried, anger making her cough even harder.

"I think you had better do it anyway," Zack said, tossing some sticks on the fire and looking across the river. "You've come too far to die here in this red mud."

Zack sure has a fine way with words, she thought as he straightened up and sloshed back to his horse.

When Addison and Snorty Watson returned, they had a big sackful of cooking utensils, the Dutch oven and the coffee pot, which was dented some but otherwise serviceable. But even the sight of what had been salvaged did not raise Carrie's spirits much. She let the men fix a pot of coffee and she drank a cup of it slowly while they talked about the passing storm. For a man who had just lost an almost new Studebaker chuck wagon worth at least seventy-five dollars on its worst day, Addison seemed mighty cheerful.

"Considering everything, we are sure lucky," he said. "Nobody drowned; we didn't lose a single Thoroughbred or Hereford. It's remarkable."

Pokey Joe Salisbury was not quite as impressed with their luck. "Well, I'm mighty glad you feel thataway, but I sure thought that I was a gonner," he muttered, sipping his coffee from one of the two tin cups they had retrieved. "I would have been, too, if I hadn't gotten ahold of that rope you threw, Mr. Wheeler."

"I'm not sure of that," Addison replied. "You and that horse of yours would probably have rolled over and over like a big log about ten times and then washed up just fine without me."

Before Pokey Joe could protest in his slow way, Zack raised a chuckle by saying, "Yeah, Pokey, I'd be interested to know how it feels to be sitting on your horse, upside down."

They laughed and Pokey Joe said, "Mighty strange; I like it right side up and breathing air a whole lot better, by gawd!"

Carrie could feel the tension bleeding out of the men, but she still felt tight inside. Tight in the lungs and tight in the stomach when she tried to raise her eyes and look at Addison, knowing he would be searching for some sign of affection and that she could offer him none.

Finally, though, she did look up. "I guess now that we are in Texas, Zack and I ought to pull out and head for Prosperity."

Zack looked at her strangely, but the expression in Addison's eyes was pure pain. He managed to say, "I've sent for a wagon and some supplies. I think you had better stay with us until you can see a doctor."

She stood up, intending to tell him that she was just

fine, but the sudden movement made her head spin and she felt so weak that her legs buckled. Addison caught her and lowered her to the ground. He looked right into her face and said, "I'm sorry, but you don't have a thing to say about the matter."

Carrie knew that it would be futile to protest. She did not want to die and she did not want to arrive on Rio's doorstep looking as if she was on her deathbed. She had visualized a thousand times how his face would change when he saw her again, how he would probably throw back his head and howl with pleasure and surprise and then open his arms for her. His mother was dead but maybe his father would be there, maybe not. It would not matter. Nothing would matter except the feel of their lips meeting again.

"All right, Mr. Wheeler," she said, "but as soon as I can travel, I'll be going to find Rio."

He nodded and a stiff mask dropped across his face, obliterating all expression. "Of course," he said, "what else could you do?"

Carrie sat before the rock fireplace and listened to the wind beat at the big ranch house. The flames danced higher, probably fed by a momentary downdraft. It was January and she had been at the Wheeler Ranch for over two months. But she was strong again, or nearly so. She glanced over at the rolltop desk, where she had watched Addison work so many evenings. He spent a good deal of time writing, doing paperwork. Carrie had never seen her own father write or do figures and there was something very reassuring about a man who could.

It was winter, and except for feeding and checking on the animals, there did not seem to be a lot to do. Com-

pared to Wyoming, Texas winters seemed almost trop-
ical. They had gotten a little snow and the wind grew
hard and cold, but the days always warmed again and
the snow never stayed on the ground. She had learned
that Pokey Joe, Snorty Watson and the two vaqueros
were his only year-round help, the rest of the cowboys
were hired early in the spring and laid off in the fall.
But many of them still ate more meals and spent more
nights at the Wheeler Ranch headquarters than they did
in Ft. Worth. And if a man was hurt or broke, Addison
always seemed to find something useful for him to do,
though it was clear he had to be creative.

The ranch house was large and comfortable, but not
richly furnished or particularly showy. Carrie had seen
bigger houses right in Cheyenne. This one was made of
logs and Addison called it a "Texas house." It was really two houses, or at least that was the way it seemed.
It had two identically sized wings, one with four bed-
rooms and a library, the other with a huge open-beamed
ceiling and this great rock fireplace that she loved. On
down the hallway were the pantry and the kitchen. Con-
necting the two wings was a roofed but otherwise open
space that Addison called a "dog trot." And though he
swore it was a blessing to sit under it in the summer,
Carrie thought it was kind of silly. In the wintertime, a
person had to pass across that twenty feet of open space
from the living room to the bedroom wing and it could
be shockingly cold at night. If I lived here, she thought,
I would enclose the danged dog trot.

But she was not going to live here; in fact, she and
Zack were leaving in the morning. It had already been
decided, though she could tell that Zack was disap-
pointed about going. He liked it here, and if it had not

been for her, he would have preferred to sleep in the bunkhouse with the vaqueros and cowboys rather than in the bedroom between her and Addison.

Darkness fell early at this time of year and Carrie had cooked a special meal of roast duck stuffed with dressing and glazed with apple sauce. She had made a blueberry pie, and though it was her best ever, no one had seemed particularly excited. In fact, as soon as it was within the realm of courtesy, Addison had excused himself and said good night. She had watched him, feeling a little hurt by his abruptness.

"And what else did you expect him to do?" Zack had demanded, his harsh words breaking through her thoughts. "You break his heart and expect a roast duck and a slice of berry pie to fix things?"

They had faced each other across the big dining room table. "Why don't *you* stay!" she had said, her voice angry.

"Because you're my sister! I got you here all the way from Wyoming and I'll be danged if I'm going to let you get killed or kidnapped by some Indian or outlaw before you get married to Rio."

"Go to bed," she had told him. "I want to leave before daylight and before we have any more hard words."

"I don't understand you, Carrie. *This* is the man you ought to marry! Not Rio Alder!"

She had trembled with rage. "I promised to marry Rio! Can't you understand anything? Love isn't something that you just turn on or off whenever you see someone else who might look better. Have you forgotten that night we ate Delmonico steaks and drank imported wine at the El Rancho in Cheyenne?"

" 'Course I haven't!"

"Well, then you must remember how Rio Alder looked you right square in the eye, man to man, and said he loved me and wanted to marry me. And we drank a toast to it. You. Me and Rio. All together."

"I'd forgotten that," he had said.

"Well, *I* haven't!"

Zack had stood up. "We leave before daybreak. Good night."

"Good night." But at the door, he had suddenly turned and yelled, "I never ate the damned Delmonico steak anyway!"

Carrie could still hear the sound of the slamming door. Zack was angry and disgusted at her, but she did not care. After she married Rio, he might be better off coming back here to live and work anyway.

Chapter Eleven

When Carrie was dressed and packed, she tiptoed down the dark hallway and paused for a moment beside Addison Wheeler's bedroom door. Then, with a sigh of resignation, she left. This was not the farewell she had wanted, but then, since Addison was in love with her, what else could she have expected? Farewells were always painful, and this one would have been particularly strained and awkward. Still, she wished that she could have left Addison on a happier note. She owed him so much and cared deeply for him.

Once outside, she looked up at the stars and then back toward the house. The bright, rectangular glow of a lantern cut across the ranch yard, telling her that Zack would probably have the horses already saddled and their gear tied down snug.

Carrie moved quickly. She was attuned to the smells

and sounds of this ranch and they were comforting. In just the few months that she had been convalescing here, the Wheeler Ranch had felt like home. It was funny, in all the years she had lived in that Wyoming soddie, it had never given her that feeling. The thought of dirt all around still made her shudder.

When Carrie entered the huge barn, Addison Wheeler was there. He smiled at her and said, "Zack and I are ready whenever you are."

Carrie was thrown off balance. "You don't need to escort us to the Alders."

"Oh," he said, matter-of-factly as he finished checking her cinch, "I know that, but I've been meaning to deliver old Jefferson Davis a Hereford bull that I promised to buy for him. I might as well get Zack to help me and save time."

Carrie's eyes widened. "You never said anything about buying a Hereford for the Alders! Why didn't you tell me that you were doing business with Rio?"

Addison finished with the cinch and dropped the stirrup down. "Because I'm not dealing with Rio," he said. "I bought a bull for Jefferson Davis, not for his son."

"It's all the same!" Carrie felt betrayed. Up to now, Addison had implied by word and action that he barely knew the Alders. Now, she realized that he knew them very well.

Addison chose to ignore her. He looked at Zack and said, "Let's get a couple of ropes on that bull and line him out. If everything goes well, we'll be in time to join the Alders for supper."

Carrie was more than miffed. She led her horse outside and mounted in the cold predawn. She rode around the barn and stopped her horse beside the lantern. In the poor light, she was surprised to see how adroitly Zack roped the big Hereford bull before Addison could add his own loop. It took both horses to drag the stubborn bull away from his harem of cows.

"Please close the gate behind us, Carrie," Addison said as he and Zack spurred their horses toward the road and tried to keep the bull moving.

Carrie dismounted, slammed the gate shut and then remounted in a huff. She checked her horse and noticed that, once they were out of the yard and headed across the ranch land, the bull quit fighting the rope and trotted along between the two horsemen just as if he knew what was expected. Unwilling to make conversation, Carrie held her horse back behind them, preferring to keep company with her anger and troubled thoughts.

She kept wondering why Addison had not mentioned being so well acquainted with the Alders. And he *had* to be well acquainted. One man did not ask another man to buy an expensive purebred bull unless he trusted that man's judgment and honesty.

Addison was jealous of Rio, she was sure of that. But she had thought him above deception.

They watched the sunrise, and slowly, the air warmed with the day. Carrie relaxed, listening to the men talk of cattle and horses while her mind reconstructed all that it could about Rio Alder. It dismayed her a little to realize that his face was no longer perfectly clear in her mind. But then, she remembered little details about him that surprised her. The way he sort of swaggered when he walked, and how he liked to comb his dark, wavy hair each time that he removed his hat. How he could wink and smile so handsomely a girl would feel her insides go warm and mushy, and how he had taught her to make love.

Remembering their lovemaking was something that she had not allowed herself to do very often; because it was so sweet and passionate, she could feel aroused just in the memory. But now that . . .

"Carrie," Addison said, twisting around in his saddle and catching her locked in the memory of Rio's powerful embrace. "Right over there on that hilltop was a famous battle between some Comanche and a company of fighting Texas Rangers. They battled for two whole days and finally both parties retreated. It's called Standoff Hill."

"Oh." Carrie tried to sound interested.

"Lot of history in this country. About two miles to the west of us is a valley filled with old buffalo bones. It's called Skull Valley. Thousands and thousands of bones are lying everywhere. The bone-pickers must have missed it."

Carrie was not interested.

Addison did not seem to notice, or if he did, he did not care. "Down south a ways is the Brazos River. Good fishing in the summertime. You ever been to Virginia, Carrie?"

"No." She wished he'd be quiet. He sounded almost cheerful.

"Beautiful state. Plantations are ruined by the Northerners, but that can't be helped. Besides, the country itself will never change. Still, after you get used to the West and its wide openness, the eastern forests seem to hem you in."

"My, my," she said, wishing he would leave her to her thoughts of Rio.

"It's the truth! I've gone back to visit, and after a few days, I feel as if I'm going to suffocate if I can't see a horizon. Still," he added, "if you haven't seen it, it's something worth visiting."

"I'll keep that in mind, Addison."

"Do that," he said in a thoughtful voice.

It was late in the afternoon when they crossed onto the Alder Ranch. Carrie's heartbeat quickened when she saw the warning sign that trespassers should keep off this private property.

"How much farther?" she asked, feeling her stomach begin to wrench up. What if Rio wasn't even there? He might have gone to Ft. Worth on business. The possibility of coming all this way and then not finding him was so depressing she dismissed it at once. He would be there waiting because he *had* to be there.

"Only about five miles," Addison said. "Their ranch house is just beyond those low hills."

Carrie stared at them, dry-mouthed with anticipation.

"You want to ride on ahead of us and meet him?" Zack asked, reading her thoughts.

"No. I . . . I've waited this long, another hour won't kill me."

But it almost did. When they finally trotted over the hills and saw the Alder Ranch sitting down in a green valley with big trees hanging over it, Carrie felt as if she knew the place by heart. Rio had drawn a sketch of it, adding his descriptions in vivid detail. He had not exaggerated its size or beauty.

The ranch house was Texas style, just like Addison's, only much larger. There were more outbuildings and she could point out the big bunkhouse, the blacksmith shop, the hay barn and the tack room. She could even point out the room where Rio slept, because he had marked it with a big X and she still had the paper.

"That's the room where we will make love every night next year," he had promised her.

Carrie took a deep breath and rode down the long, green hills into the ranch with Zack, Addison and the Hereford bull.

Their arrival was announced well ahead of time by a pair of loudly barking black and white dogs. It was supper time, but Carrie had no appetite. In fact, she felt half sick with anxiety.

Cowboys moseyed out of the bunkhouse, carrying their plates and unfinished cups of coffee, curious about the new bull and the visitors. Carrie recognized a few, but none of them acted as if they recognized her. When the front porch of the ranch house banged open, she caught her breath, but it was not Rio. Instead, a large man stepped out and ran his fingers through his silver hair. He came forward to greet them and he was smiling.

"Howdy, Addison!" the man bellowed. "So you finally got around to bringing me that Hereford bull you promised!"

"Yes, sir, Jefferson. Like him?"

The old Texas rancher circled the bull, studying him from every angle with an entirely critical eye. "Kinda sawed-off, ain't he?"

"Yeah," Addison said agreeably, "but look at the size of his shoulder and rump muscles. He'll have more and better steaks and roasts hanging on him and his offspring than any two of our longhorns."

"Think he's tall enough to mount a longhorn cow?"

"He's already proved it more than once on my place," Addison said.

Carrie's cheeks colored. She struggled to get her breath. Her heart was pounding and her mouth felt dry. She could not tear her eyes away from the ranch house door.

"Jefferson, I'd like you to meet two friends of mine. This is Miss Carrie Bennett and this is her brother, Zack. Miss Bennett came all the way from around Cheyenne, Wyoming, to see Rio."

Jefferson Davis seemed about to say something, but he decided against it. "Miss Bennett, step down, you have indeed come a long way."

He looked gracious but puzzled. Carrie felt a wild surge of dread. She climbed down from her horse and clung to the animal a moment for support. Seeing her face, Zack came to her side and she was grateful.

"Young lady, why do you want to see my son?"

She was so scared she had to swallow a couple of times. "He . . . uh, we . . ." She couldn't say it. She turned to Zack, eyes pleading.

Zack straightened. "Rio and Carrie, well, they . . . they fell in love and are getting married. Rio promised her."

The old rancher blinked. He glanced at Addison as if seeking some answer.

Carrie spoke up. "We . . . we *stayed* together in Cheyenne, Mr. Alder. I guess this is kind of a shock to you, but it couldn't be as much of a shock as it was to my own father. That's why I came. To be married as we planned. Is he . . . is he still alive!"

The rancher looked deep into her eyes. Satisfied, he twisted away and shouted, "Rio! Get out here!"

Carrie swung back around, and when her Rio stepped outside, she almost swooned. He had not changed a bit.

He was still the most beautiful man she had ever seen and seeing him now filled her with such joy she flung herself across the yard and into his arms.

"I love you!" she sobbed.

His body stiffened. His hands pushed her away and held her out at arms reach. He looked to his pa and the other men. "What the hell is going on?" he shouted. "What is *she* doing here!"

Carrie recoiled. "Rio, you said we were to be married. You said you loved me!"

"She's crazy, Pa! I knew her only a couple of days. She's just some poor sodbuster's daughter. She's a nothing!"

Zack felt his guts turn to ice. He saw his sister stagger. He looked at Addison and then at Mr. Alder and he saw nothing but disgust.

Zack rushed to his sister and grabbed her. She felt as if she had been carved out of stone. She stood half bent, her hands over her face. He could hear her breathing hard and making little sounds way down in her throat.

"Rio, goddamn you, you're lying!" Jefferson Davis Alder shouted. "Look at what you're doing to her!"

"Pa! Ask any of the boys who were there in Wyoming with me. They'll tell you she's nothing. Why, I had three other women in Cheyenne and . . ."

Carrie screamed, a high, tortured sound that made Zack's hair stand up on end. She grabbed his old Navy Colt and then, before he could move to stop her, she shot Rio twice at point-blank range in the chest. He staggered and Zack saw his head shake and then he collapsed on the porch, dead before he hit the boards.

Zack lunged at Carrie who turned the gun on herself. "No!" he shouted, batting wildly at her wrist.

The Colt exploded once more and Carrie fell into his arms.

"A doctor!" Zack bellowed helplessly as he felt the warm, wet blood emptying from her.

Everyone but Addison was shouting. He scooped her up and rushed inside, laid her down on a cowhide sofa and ripped his own shirt apart, then stuffed it into the bullet wound high up in her shoulder.

Zack heard two horses thunder out of the ranch yard. He twisted around to see Mr. Alder lift Rio and then carry him inside and through a doorway to disappear in grief.

"Is she going to live?"

Addison looked up at him. "I don't know," he whispered. "She might if she wants to."

"She doesn't want to anymore. She wants to die."

Addison nodded. He bent his head and wept.

Chapter Twelve

Spring roundup on the Wheeler Ranch was something that had given Zack all the roping and cattle working he'd needed to earn the title of cowboy. Not that he would ever be as good with a lariat as Ignacio or Ramon, but he was already Snorty Watson's equal and that was no small potatoes.

Now, after over four hundred miles of trailing long-horn cattle north, Zack and Addison Wheeler rode stirrup to stirrup toward Ellsworth, Kansas. Zack sat tall in the saddle, like a man born on a horse instead of one destined to trod behind a plow. Between his legs was a chestnut gelding, one of the thoroughbred crosses that Addison had let him buy out of his wages. The animal was lean and hardened by the long cattle drive—like its rider.

They could see the outline of Ellsworth on the northern horizon. As they galloped nearer, Zack decided not much had changed about that rail town since he and Carrie had departed from it last autumn. The town appeared to have neither grown nor diminished.

I'm the only thing that's changed, he thought.

A strong, free wind was blowing off the Colorado plateau and carrying the scent of grass and trees all the way from the Rocky Mountains. Zack screwed his Caldwell Stetson down tighter and let his horse gallop crossways to the wind. He glanced over at the man beside him and saw that Addison was smiling.

They had reason to smile. Theirs was the first Texas trail herd to arrive at Ellsworth, Kansas, this spring and they knew that they would get a fine price for their beef. And next year, when the Hereford blood started to show in their market cattle, they would get an even better price.

"Let's have a celebration drink at the Alamo Saloon," Addison yelled, "then we'll let the buyers have a go at us!"

Zack nodded agreeably.

"I'll race you to the town limits!" Addison yelled. "Loser buys the first drink and then dinner!"

Zack let his horse have its head. The two geldings were half-brothers and perfectly matched. Addison's palomino flattened its ears and burst ahead by a length, but within a mile Zack had closed the distance and the two horses were running neck and neck, gobbling up the prairie between themselves and Ellsworth in huge strides.

"Woo-weee!" Zack shouted into the wind.

Beside him, Addison let out a wild Texas yell as their horses streaked past the town limit sign and skidded around the corner by Hiram Dudley's Livery.

It was a draw, though Zack figured the palomino was still the faster horse and that maybe Addison had eased up on his reins a mite during the last hundred yards.

Several townspeople and merchants made a big show of coming out to wave and extend their greetings as they dismounted in front of the Alamo Saloon. They wanted to know where the cowboys were and how many herds were following up from Texas this year. After Addison assured them there would be at least as many cattle coming to Ellsworth as last year, they were very happy.

Under his breath, Addison said, "Zack, these towns-folk always greet the first few Texas trail herds as if we were their salvation, which I expect we are. The boys will have drinks on the house and everything. But by September, when the stockyards are filled and the cow-boys have treed Ellsworth one too many times, they'll treat us worse than bubonic plague carriers."

"Well," Zack said, "let's take advantage of the sit-uation and enjoy a well-earned chicken dinner."

They had already decided that it would be chicken; a man got tired of eating beef after following a steer's rear end for over four hundred miles.

They had three drinks each instead of the one, and they were all on the house and so strong that Zack was feeling a little giddy by the time Addison took his arm and led him out of the saloon to eat dinner.

"How much did that first buyer offer you?" Zack asked.

"Thirty dollars a head, sight unseen."

"How about the second one?"

"Thirty-one." Addison steered him into the Partridge Café which boasted having the best chicken dinners in

Kansas. "But I figure that I can get thirty-five by Wednesday. After that, the next herd will be here and the price will drop a good three dollars."

A pretty young waitress about Zack's age came over and took their order. She could not seem to stop smiling at the tall, youthful cowboy and Zack smiled back with real interest.

"You sure showed her all your teeth," Addison said confidentially. "If you was a horse, I'd buy you."

Zack blushed. "I'm going to miss all the teasin'," he said.

"Well then, why don't you change your mind and send a letter instead of riding clear up to Cheyenne? Do that and I think that waitress might even favor you with more than a smile," Addison said thoughtfully.

Zack looked at the man across from him and his smile died. "I got to tell my folks in person about Carrie. A letter or telegram won't do."

"I understand. When are you leaving?"

"When I finish with this chicken dinner."

"You could take the Kansas Pacific Railroad to Denver and then buy a ticket up to Cheyenne on the Denver Pacific. Be easier and faster."

Zack shook his head. "Me and Carrie rode from here to Denver on the train. I'll stick to horseback this time. Besides," Zack added, stretching out his long legs and trying not to scratch up the floor too bad with his spurs, "I guess I always dreamed of riding up to our old homestead on a horse looking like a cowboy instead of a sodbuster."

Addison looked at him intently. "Sodbuster. That term used to bother you and Carrie a great deal, didn't it?"

"Yeah," Zack admitted, "I hated the word, though it was an accurate enough description."

"When I first got to know Carrie on the way down to Texas, she used to talk about sod houses. She'd get upset just thinking about them."

"She hated them worse than I ever did. But then women generally do. They have to try to keep the danged things clean, cook in them, wash and all the other things. A man, he leaves in the morning and is gone all day. Me and Pa worked so many hours that we could have slept in a bear cave and not noticed the difference."

Their meal came and they ate it with great satisfaction. And when it was over and the final details had been rehashed once more, Zack said good-bye to Addison Wheeler. He rode northwest out of Ellsworth on a course that would clip the corner of Colorado and bring him across the plains to Cheyenne and the old homestead.

The days passed uneventfully. He saw few riders and he traveled without fear or hurry. He had thought about his ma and pa for nearly a whole year and knew that his arrival might cause them pain. That could not be helped. Pa had driven Carrie away. Zack now believed what had happened to Carrie was inevitable. Ma and Pa needed to be told.

He rode into Cheyenne and tied up his horse in front of Dr. Holstetter's office. Mr. Ferris, the town banker, looked at Zack, but his quizzical expression said he didn't quite place the face with the cowboy. Since Mr. Ferris had always looked down his nose at sodbusters, Zack did not enlighten him.

Inside the office, he was greeted by a boy whom the doctor had paid a nickel to watch things and relay messages.

Zack took twenty dollars from his vest pocket and handed it to the boy. "You give this to Doc and tell him that Zachariah Bennett paid it, on account of what he did for my ma and pa last year."

The boy's eyes widened as he looked up at the tall cowboy. "You're Zack Bennett?"

"That's right. The doctor let my ma and pa stay here in the little house out in back."

"She still lives there."

It was Zack's turn to be surprised. "Is she with Pa?"

The boy shook his head. "Your Pa, he still lives out at his homestead. But he's sick."

"Then why don't he come here to live with Ma?"

"I guess he just won't," the boy said. "But your Ma is doing fine. She's generally helpin' the doc and taking care of the place. Right now, she's off doing some shopping for the doc."

Zack removed his Stetson and ran his fingers through his long hair, then he turned to leave.

"Say, mister, you want me to tell your ma you came by?"

"Nope," he decided out loud, "I would rather surprise her."

Zack came walking back down the street an hour later with two bundles tucked under his arm. He tied one behind his bedroll on the leggy chestnut and the other one he carried down the alley to give to his mother.

When her door opened to his knock, she just stared at him for a moment before a small cry of joy burst from her. She reached up on the tips of her toes and he swept her off the floor and swung her around completely, forgetting that she shouldn't be handled so roughly.

"Zacky," she whispered, taking in his hat, boots and the same yellow bandanna that Miss Annie Norton once had given him. "You're a cowboy fer sure, just like you always said you'd be! My, but you look tall and handsome!"

"You look good yourself," he said, meaning it. "City life must be agreeing with you. But what about Pa?"

His mother looked away quickly. "He hurt his back last year and we almost killed ourselves getting in the winter wheat crop. Dr. Holstetter asked us both to live here for free and just give him a little help. But your pa . . ."

"I know," he said. "You don't have to explain."

"Zack, I swear, without Carrie, I couldn't take another winter out there. Not alone!"

She buried her face against his shoulder and Zack felt her guilt and her pain, how much it had cost her to leave Pa out on the homestead. He knew she was pleading with him for understanding.

Zack put his arms around her thin shoulders. He handed her the package. "It's for you," he said. "I want you to wear it tomorrow when I take you to church."

She opened it to find a beautiful, flowered dress, a pair of shoes and the fanciest bonnet in all of Cheyenne. Tears filled her eyes. "I can't wear such prettiness," she sniffled. "I'm too old and too washed out anymore."

Zack kissed her cheek and wiped away the tears with his yellow bandanna. "You just be quiet and be ready to go to church with me tomorrow morning in that outfit," he said gently.

When she nodded and smiled, he got up to leave. "I'm going out to see the place and to talk to Pa."

"Zack, he's real bitter about you and Carrie. Real

195

bitter. He can't do much work and he ain't struck any water yet. Guess he'll lose that old place."

"I already guessed it might turn out that way," Zack said.

She stood up and came to him and he saw fear clouding her eyes. "What happened to Carrie? Tell me the truth. Did that young Rio Alder marry her like he swore he would?"

"No, Ma. He lied to her so she killed him. There was a trial, but it was clear to everyone in Prosperity—even Jefferson Davis Alder—that Rio got what was coming. Carrie was in jail less than a month before they set her free. A couple of months ago, she married a man named Addison Wheeler. They're going to have a baby around Christmas time."

"Praise be to God!" she cried, breaking out in fresh tears and clapping her hands together with joy. "Oh, praise be to God! And will she live in a *wood* house?"

He grinned. "A fine one, Ma. With a big fireplace and windows in every direction. It doesn't even have a root cellar."

"Oh, thanks be to God!" Ma wailed, breaking into fresh tears.

When she stopped weeping, Zack left her and rode out to the homestead.

Nothing about the place had changed. The spring grass still waved in the breeze and the golden winter wheat was coming up about half as fast as it would have in Kansas or Nebraska.

Pa was sitting on the porch in a rocking chair and he looked a hundred years old. When he saw a Texas cowboy come riding across his quarter section of land, he shuffled inside and came out with his rifle.

Zack reined up in the yard, studying every inch of the soddie and the yard. The tall pole where Red Rooster had perched and clung through so many storms was gone and so was the bird. The livestock corral was broken down; the other animals were gone, too.

"It's me, Pa." He did not dismount.

Adolph Bennett lowered his rifle. He studied the sleek chestnut and the tall young man who rode it. "You're not my son," he whispered. "You're the son of Satan and you have ridden up from the depths of everlasting hell."

"No, I haven't," Zack said quietly. "I'm Zachariah Bennett and you're my father. Carrie is married and living in Texas with a good man."

"Get off my land, you devil!"

Zack nodded quietly. He rode over to the corner of the house, bent low in the saddle and scooped up a shovel.

"You put that back or so help me God, I'll kill you, Devil!"

Zack's face was set and pale as he rode the chestnut away. He wondered if his father would kill him and expected he just might, for the man had always had a murderous temper.

But there was no shot, and when Zack reached the old well hole where he'd last worked, he dismounted. He stripped down to his underclothes, still hearing his father's shouts and yet not really hearing him at all anymore.

He opened the package and climbed into a pair of new bib overalls. They were stiff and very blue. He removed his pointed-toed cowboy boots and replaced them with round-toed work boots. He climbed down into the half-finished well, and while the leggy chestnut began to graze under the prairie sky, Zack started digging again.

POWDER RIVER

Gary McCarthy

Utah in the mid-1800s is truly wild, a land still largely untamed by law and settled by only the strongest—and bravest—souls. Few men have the courage to survive. And even fewer women. Despite the odds, Katie remains. A young, single woman, she is determined to raise her child and manage her sheep ranch without the help of any man...though a powerful cattleman, a ranch hand and an Eastern gentleman each have different ideas.

___4408-0 $5.50 US/$6.50 CAN

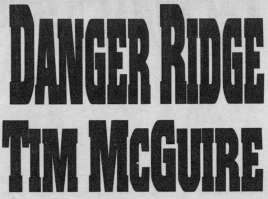

DANGER RIDGE
TIM McGUIRE

Clay Cole is a man with a shadowy past. Most folks know he is good with a gun, but that is all they know. Very few know the Army is out to court-martial him for something he didn't do. And even fewer know he has accepted a job to lead a young bride along a dangerous trail to meet her husband. But the men who do know it are aiming to kill him and the woman along the trail. And the easiest place to do that is the treacherous sort few men make it through—the place the Westerners call danger ridge.

___4410-2 $4.50 US/$5.50 CAN

Dorchester Publishing Co., Inc.
P.O. Box 6640
Wayne, PA 19087-8640

Please add $1.75 for shipping and handling for the first book and $.50 for each book thereafter. NY, NYC, and PA residents, please add appropriate sales tax. No cash, stamps, or C.O.D.s. All orders shipped within 6 weeks via postal service book rate. Canadian orders require $2.00 extra postage and must be paid in U.S. dollars through a U.S. banking facility.

Name_____
Address_____
City_____State_____Zip_____
I have enclosed $_____ in payment for the checked book(s).
Payment <u>must</u> accompany all orders. ☐ Please send a free catalog.
CHECK OUT OUR WEBSITE! www.dorchesterpub.com

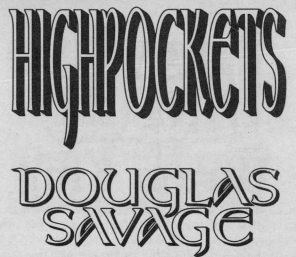

HIGHPOCKETS

DOUGLAS SAVAGE

In the autumn of his days, Highpockets stumbles upon a half-frozen immigrant boy, nearly dead and terrified after being separated from his family's wagon train. For one long, brutal winter Highpockets tries to teach the boy all he needs to know to survive in a land as dangerous as it is beautiful. But will it be enough to see both man and boy through the deadly trial that is still to come?

___4400-5 $3.99 US/$4.99 CAN

Dorchester Publishing Co., Inc.
P.O. Box 6640
Wayne, PA 19087-8640

Please add $1.75 for shipping and handling for the first book and $.50 for each book thereafter. NY, NYC, and PA residents, please add appropriate sales tax. No cash, stamps, or C.O.D.s. All orders shipped within 6 weeks via postal service book rate. Canadian orders require $2.00 extra postage and must be paid in U.S. dollars through a U.S. banking facility.

Name_____
Address_____
City_____ State_____ Zip_____
I have enclosed $_____ in payment for the checked book(s).
Payment <u>must</u> accompany all orders. ❑ Please send a free catalog.
CHECK OUT OUR WEBSITE! www.dorchesterpub.com

DARK TRAIL

Hiram King

When the War Between the States was finally over, many men returned from battle only to find their homes destroyed and their families scattered to the wind. Bodie Johnson is one of those men. But while some families fled before advancing armies, the Johnson family was packed up like cattle and shipped west—on a slave train. With only that information to go on, Bodie sets out to find whatever remains of his family. And he will do it. Because no matter how vast the West is, no matter what stands in his way, Bodie knows one thing—the Johnsons will survive.

____4418-8 $5.50 US/$6.50 CAN

Dorchester Publishing Co., Inc.
P.O. Box 6640
Wayne, PA 19087-8640

Please add $1.75 for shipping and handling for the first book and $.50 for each book thereafter. NY, NYC, and PA residents, please add appropriate sales tax. No cash, stamps, or C.O.D.s. All orders shipped within 6 weeks via postal service book rate. Canadian orders require $2.00 extra postage and must be paid in U.S. dollars through a U.S. banking facility.

Name_____
Address_____
City_____State_____Zip_____
I have enclosed $_____ in payment for the checked book(s).
Payment __must__ accompany all orders. ☐ Please send a free catalog.
    CHECK OUT OUR WEBSITE! www.dorchesterpub.com

BLACK RIVER FALLS
ED GORMAN

"Gorman's writing is strong, fast and sleek as a bullet. He's one of the best."
—Dean Koontz

Who would want to kill a beautiful young woman like Alison...and why? But whatever happens, nineteen-year-old Ben Tyler swears that he will protect her. It hasn't been easy for Ben—the boy the other kids always picked on. But then Ben finds Alison and at last things are going his way...Until one day he learns a secret so ugly that his entire life is changed forever. A secret that threatens to destroy everyone he loves. A secret as dark and dangerous as the tumbling waters of Black River Falls.

"Gorman has a way of getting into his characters and they have a way of getting into you."
—Robert Block, author of *Psycho*

——4265-7 $4.99 US/$5.99 CAN

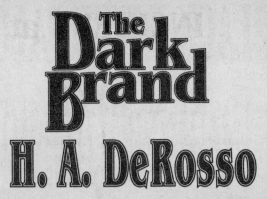

The Dark Brand

H. A. DeRosso

Driscoll made a mistake and he's paying for it. They stuck him in a cell—with a man condemned to hang the next morning. Driscoll learns how his cellmate robbed a bank and killed a man...and how the money was never recovered. But he never learns where the money is. After Driscoll serves his time and drifts back into town, he learns that the loot is still hidden, and that just about everyone thinks the condemned man told Driscoll where it is buried before he died. Suddenly it seems everybody wants that money— enough to kill for it.

___4412-9 $4.50 US/$5.50 CAN

Dorchester Publishing Co., Inc.
P.O. Box 6640
Wayne, PA 19087-8640

Please add $1.75 for shipping and handling for the first book and $.50 for each book thereafter. NY, NYC, and PA residents, please add appropriate sales tax. No cash, stamps, or C.O.D.s. All orders shipped within 6 weeks via postal service book rate. Canadian orders require $2.00 extra postage and must be paid in U.S. dollars through a U.S. banking facility.

Name_____
Address_____
City_____State_____Zip_____
I have enclosed $_____ in payment for the checked book(s).
Payment <u>must</u> accompany all orders. ❏ Please send a free catalog.
CHECK OUT OUR WEBSITE! www.dorchesterpub.com

INCIDENT at

ROBERT J. CONLEY

The Sacred Hill. It rose above the land, drawing men to it like a beacon. But the men who came each had their own dreams. There is Zeno Bond, the settler who dreams of land and empire. There is Mat McDonald, captain of the steamship *John Hart*, heading the looming war between the Spanish and the Americans. And there is Walker, the Cherokee warrior called by a vision he cannot deny—a vision of life, death...and destiny.

___4396-3 $4.50 US/$5.50 CAN

Dorchester Publishing Co., Inc.
P.O. Box 6640
Wayne, PA 19087-8640

Please add $1.75 for shipping and handling for the first book and $.50 for each book thereafter. NY, NYC, and PA residents, please add appropriate sales tax. No cash, stamps, or C.O.D.s. All orders shipped within 6 weeks via postal service book rate. Canadian orders require $2.00 extra postage and must be paid in U.S. dollars through a U.S. banking facility.

Name_____
Address_____
City_____ State_____ Zip_____
I have enclosed $_____ in payment for the checked book(s).
Payment <u>must</u> accompany all orders. ❏ Please send a free catalog.
CHECK OUT OUR WEBSITE! www.dorchesterpub.com

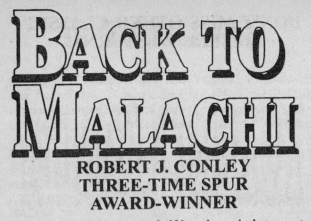

BACK TO MALACHI

ROBERT J. CONLEY
THREE-TIME SPUR
AWARD-WINNER

Charlie Black is a young half-breed caught between two worlds. He is drawn to the promise of the white man's wealth, but torn by his proud heritage as a Cherokee. Charlie's pretty young fiancée yearns for the respectability of a Christian marriage and baptized children. But Charlie can't forsake his two childhood friends, Mose and Henry Pathkiller, who live in the hills with an old full-blooded Indian named Malachi. When Mose runs afoul of the law, Charlie has to choose between the ways of his fiancée and those of his friends and forefathers. He has to choose between surrender and bloodshed.

___4277-0 $3.99 US/$4.99 CAN

Dorchester Publishing Co., Inc.
P.O. Box 6640
Wayne, PA 19087-8640